"Clearl[y] ... origina[l] ... [stakes]," Roman went on. "If anything, I want you more than ever."

"Same," Sable murmured "That is, I agree about the heat level. Still...hot."

"Hey. We don't have to act on it just because it's there. I'm going to be with you through this pregnancy whether you want to share my bed again or not."

"It's just the chemistry is so strong. What if a return to intimacy makes it impossible to make objective decisions? The stakes are higher than ever now, so I don't want to make a bad call about what happens between us."

"I admit that I don't *like* that answer, but I respect the hell out of you for it."

"You do?"

"Hell yes. You're protecting our future relationship as parents. The only answer is that we wait."

* * *

A Nine-Month Temptation by Joanne Rock is part of the Brooklyn Nights series.

Dear Reader,

My oldest son moved to Brooklyn a few years ago, living with roommates while he established his career. His living situation reminded me of my own summers spent in Manhattan with friends, and soon, story ideas for modern New York roommates kept chirping in my ear. It is with great pleasure I introduce you to the first of my Brooklyn Nights heroines, Sable Cordero.

Sable's dream job as a fashion stylist is upended by a one-night stand with her boss that leads to a surprise pregnancy. She'll do anything to protect her baby—but could that mean trusting powerful Roman Zayn to be...a daddy?

I hope you enjoy this trip to New York City, where dreams are made and the Brooklyn nights are sizzling!

Happy reading,

Joanne Rock

JOANNE ROCK

A NINE-MONTH TEMPTATION

HARLEQUIN
DESIRE

HARLEQUIN®
DESIRE™

ISBN-13: 978-1-335-23297-7

A Nine-Month Temptation

Harlequin Enterprises ULC
22 Adelaide St. West, 40th Floor
Toronto, Ontario M5H 4E3, Canada
www.Harlequin.com

Printed in U.S.A.

Joanne Rock credits her decision to write romance after a book she picked up during a flight delay engrossed her so thoroughly that she didn't mind at all when her flight was delayed two more times. Giving her readers the chance to escape into another world has motivated her to write over eighty books for a variety of Harlequin series.

Books by Joanne Rock

Harlequin Desire

Brooklyn Nights

A Nine-Month Temptation

Dynasties: Mesa Falls

The Rebel
The Rival
Rule Breaker
Heartbreaker
The Rancher
The Heir

Visit her Author Profile page at Harlequin.com, or joannerock.com, for more titles.

You can also find Joanne Rock on Facebook, along with other Harlequin Desire authors, at Facebook.com/harlequindesireauthors!

In loving memory of my favorite NYC roommate, Rebecca Schaeffer.

One

Best. Job. Ever.

Sable Cordero sipped the fine champagne and toasted herself in the full-length mirror at the Zayn Designs studio in Manhattan, where she'd been working as a stylist for three months. What other line of work would give a backwoods Louisiana divorcée with more ambition than savings the opportunity to drape herself in haute couture from the most lauded new brand of the year? She didn't own the sample-sized dress, of course. It was far beyond her financial means. But tonight she got to wear the silk work of art for the sake of a social media video she was creating after hours. The designer, Marcel Zayn, had been fully supportive of her wish to help develop content for the brand, not even blinking at the idea of her remaining late in the studio unsupervised.

And damn, but she appreciated his faith in her. At twenty-nine years old, Sable was older than anyone else employed by the fashion house, except for the designer himself. She couldn't be more thankful for the opportunity to chase her dream of being a stylist after the brief detour of an unhappy marriage.

She'd been given a second chance at life. One she would not take for granted.

Once upon a time, she'd nabbed a fashion degree from Louisiana State, but she'd gotten sidetracked by a smooth-talking political science major who convinced her she wanted to share his dream instead of her own. In hindsight, she could hardly be surprised that he moved on when she stopped fulfilling his vision of what he wanted in a wife. She'd learned the hard way that some men just marry women as placeholders, human mirrors to reflect back what they want to see.

Sable was mostly cured of the bitterness surrounding her ex. Nevertheless, she cranked up the stereo volume as Beyoncé sang about putting middle fingers up and saying, "boy, bye."

She couldn't be bitter after scoring this dream job. She might be living hand-to-mouth for a while in the Brooklyn apartment she shared with three other women, but at least she had a great place to call home.

Sable danced around the hardwood floor in bare feet. Tonight, she was filming after hours, incorporating the champagne brand that had approached Zayn about some sponsored ads—a budget-friendly way to extend the fledgling design house's marketing reach. She didn't need to be model-gorgeous since she was filming herself from the back, where the dramatic ribbon ties of the neckline fell over mostly bare skin until they grazed the sexy-as-hell silk that wrapped her hips.

Careful not to spill her drink, Sable went around the Tribeca loft space making sure all her props were positioned for the series of short videos. She'd culled the designer's most visually interesting furnishings, dragging them all into the open section of the loft where she'd walk among them in her dress. She'd flipped on a few spotlights and filled in the dark areas with a couple of borrowed floor lamps. It wasn't high tech, but it would get the job done. Her video concept wasn't super fancy, either. She planned to film the same basic movements twice—once tonight while wearing the black version of the silk dress, and again during daylight hours clad in the same dramatic dress in white. Then she'd interpose the segments in editing.

She was almost ready. She just needed a little more mojo to fuel her attempt at a catwalk swagger.

"Cheers to me." Sable lifted the flute to her lips again, savoring the way the bubbles tickled her nose before she downed another sip.

She wanted the champagne bottle to be half-empty in her video, and she *obviously* couldn't dump the contents of a ridiculously expensive vintage down the drain. The only appropriate action was drinking it herself. Besides, she needed the confidence boost those bubbles provided since the silk fit like a second skin and she was about to film her ass in unforgiving high definition. Alcohol and Queen B on the stereo were both required, considering the Zayn videos were getting over a hundred thousand views.

And yeah, maybe she'd opted to put herself out there tonight in the latest video as her final middle finger to her ex. She'd gotten a call from her mother today that he was expecting a baby with his new wife, the woman who'd taken her place even before Sable had realized she wasn't wanted anymore.

While she no longer resented him moving on, she resented the hell out of him leaving her because of her inability to give him a baby. She'd tried. Yes, it had hurt her that she hadn't been successful in keeping their marriage afloat. But what hurt more was the memory of her miscarriage, which had filled her with a deep sense of loss. So it was galling that her ex had replaced her with someone more fertile.

That warranted the badass babe music and all the boss-woman attitude she could bring to this dress. Sable slid on the sky-high stilettos guaranteed to make any woman's legs look delicious. She hadn't felt sexy in a long, long time.

Unbidden, an image of Roman Zayn came into her mind. Roman was the design house's owner, Marcel's older brother, and the power behind the throne. Or maybe Sable just saw him that way because Roman's brand of tall, dark and brooding had slid past her professional reserve and done something wicked to her insides the lone time they'd met. They'd only exchanged a few words during her first week on the job before he returned to LA, where he ran Zayn Equity, a global wealth management company. Yet the man's probing stare had stripped her bare and sent her sensual imagination off and running.

It had been silly, really. Just a fanciful turn of her thoughts that would never come to anything since Roman had little to do with the day-to-day workings of the fashion house. But that moment alone with him when he'd asked about her experience   in fashion, of course—had been the last time she'd felt a hint of feminine power.

So she let that memory wash over her as she took

a deep breath, finger hovering over the record button on her phone where it rested in a cradle on the tripod.

Hell yes, she was moving on. Chasing her dream. In three, two, one…

Roman Zayn heard the music as soon as his black Town Car pulled up outside the Vestry Street building where his brother worked. Considering the Zayn Designs loft was on the seventh floor, that struck Roman as…excessive. But definitely not out of character for Marcel, the family black sheep to everyone but Roman. Marcel lived by his own lights and Roman admired the hell out of him for it, which was why he'd agreed to be his business partner. Marcel might not have Roman's financial know-how, but the man knew clothing.

Besides, Marcel had been there for Roman during the darkest year of his life. He'd been the only family member to show up for him with more than just platitudes during the hell he'd gone through when his wife died. Roman owed him for that.

But as much as he loved Marcel, he also understood his brother's tendencies to overspend in order to bring his art to life. Roman had committed to putting in an appearance at the atelier as often as possible to keep the design house within budget while they found an audience that could sustain the kind of business Marcel envisioned. Roman hoped the pop anthem blaring out the seventh-floor window at 10:00 p.m. meant his brother was working overtime toward that goal. He hadn't planned to meet with him personally tonight, thinking he'd duck into the small suite attached to the workshop and catch a few hours of sleep before intercepting his brother first thing in the morning. He'd been trying to avoid seeing anyone else at the studio.

Namely the newly hired stylist Roman had met on his last trip to New York. The Southern siren who'd ignited a flashfire of lust with just a few words spoken in her molasses-thick drawl.

He'd stayed away from Zayn Designs longer than usual to avoid her. Roman didn't deny himself feminine companionship since his wife's death. But he preferred to slake that thirst with women who didn't stir quite so…much. Curvaceous, delectable Sable had "too much" stamped across her perpetually bee-stung lips.

If Roman could speak with Marcel tonight, he could leave early for his other meetings tomorrow morning before anyone else arrived at the studio.

"Have a good night," Roman called to the driver through the open window after he got out.

Stepping into the building's brick archway, he swiped his keycard and opened a wrought iron door to access the elevator behind it. He noticed the sound of the music was fainter here as he unearthed a second security key for the elevator.

Once inside the industrial-sized lift, Roman loosened his tie. He'd kept it on for video conferencing during the flight from LA, but his brother would only harangue him about his too-conservative clothes. No doubt, the customer base for a wealth management firm was a world away from high fashion. His shirt, at least, had been made by his brother. Sure, Marcel designed more women's garments than men's, but his clothes for men were fantastic, from the mother-of-pearl buttons to the French seams and custom tailoring.

Roman stuffed his tie into his briefcase as the elevator door opened onto the loft. R&B music made the floor vibrate, the horns blaring and drums thumping as loud as in any dance club. The lights shone brightly in the center of the work area, while the edges of the room remained in shadow.

But it wasn't the light or the music that hit his senses like an assault.

That honor went to the woman strutting away from him in a black silk dress that molded to her curves like it had been poured over her. Her lustrous, dark hair was piled haphazardly on her head, a braid coiled around the mass like an afterthought to keep it in place. The dress had no back. Zero. The fabric only covered the soft swell of her ass, the silk cupping the bared dimples at the base of her spine as if to highlight that undeniably sexy feature.

Two thick ribbons cascaded from a knot at her neck to sway between her shoulder blades. As she moved, her hips rolled in a come-hither rhythm so seductive he found himself following in her wake even from ten yards away. A champagne flute dangled carelessly from her fingertips as she wove her way between stylized dress forms and the kitschy busts of composers that Marcel collected. She moved among them like they were adoring lovers, caressing a cheek here, bumping hips with a mannequin there.

She was so sexy she took his breath away, his pulse pounding in time with each step of her stilettos.

Tap. Tap. Tap.

How had the beat synced up? He wanted to catch her. Pull those teasing hips against him.

Right up until she paused to cast a sultry glance over one shoulder. And promptly screamed at seeing him.

The champagne glass shattered on the hardwood.

Damn.

It was *her*. Recognizing the very woman he'd been hoping to avoid, Roman regained his faculties at once.

"It's just me," he assured her, moving toward the stereo system on the shelf between two of the huge arched windows overlooking the street. Dialing down the volume, he turned toward Sable, the woman who'd populated far too many fantasies since his one and only meeting with her. "Roman," he reminded her.

He couldn't help feeling the flash of annoyance that she was staring at him like she'd seen a ghost. The thought of her forgetting him when she'd made an indelible impression on him was a definite kick to the ego. Not that it mattered.

"Of course I remember you." She hastened to speak, possibly hearing the irritation in his voice. "I'm sorry." She started to take a halting step, her movements jerky. Was she embarrassed? "I wasn't expecting anyone," she rushed to explain, color flooding her cheeks.

Seeing that she was about to step on glass, he crossed the floor to help her. Somehow, that meant lifting her off her feet to remove her from the danger. Roman realized how unwise that decision had been the moment his fingers encircled her almost-naked waist. His fingers caressed bare skin while his thumbs pressed into the black silk just above her hips. For a scant second, her breasts grazed his chest as he picked her up.

He didn't want to let go. Not when he could feel the tight points of her nipples brush against him. Not when he heard the swift intake of her breath, felt the rush of air along the heated skin at his neck, saw the flash of awareness in her hazel eyes. Hell no, he didn't want to release her.

Which was why he forced himself to put her down, prying his fingers free from the magnetic force that was her gorgeous body, then jamming them into his pants pockets where he balled them into fists.

She looked up at him, confusion in her gaze as if she had no idea why he'd picked her up. Or maybe she was unsure why he let her go. And didn't that thought mess with his head? He ground his teeth together and brusquely said, "I need a broom."

Stalking away from her, he went to find one to clean up the glass, knowing he sounded rude but needing to keep his hands busy. Definitely needing his hands off her.

"I can get it," she called, following him into the tiny galley kitchen someone had added to the loft in a long-ago renovation. "I made the mess. I can certainly clean it up."

From the softness of her footfall, he guessed she'd taken off her shoes. And it disturbed him how acutely attuned his senses were to her movement.

He could only brace himself and hold his breath when she leaned past him to reach for the broom and dustpan in the recess between the cabinets. The scent of her hair tickled his nose, something lemony and sweet.

Her hip bumped his and she murmured, "Excuse me." She lifted her face to his again. "I'm just so mortified to have screamed like some ninny in a horror movie. I'm Sable, by the way, in case you don't remember. Marcel never mentioned you were arriving tonight, so I thought I was alone."

Roman's pulse ticked in his temple as he stared down at her, willing himself not to touch her again. Seeing her now reawakened every hot fantasy he'd had about her since they'd met three months ago. She was still too *much*, the feelings she awakened stirring something that felt more ominous than simple lust. And yet…what if acting on the lust deflated things back down to a manageable level? He was so keyed up he was tempted to try, except that she worked for Marcel.

Hell, technically, she worked for *him*. So taking a taste of her was out of the question. He needed to shake off this spell she had him under and take control of the situation.

"I remember you." He let that sink in for a moment before he took the broom out of her hands and charged toward the broken glass. He'd help her clean up and then he'd get a hotel. "And Marcel didn't expect me. The fault is mine for not warning him. Tonight, it never occurred to me that anyone but him would be here at this hour. When I heard the music outside, I assumed he was working late."

He tackled the glass shards with a vengeance, drawing the bristles over the hardwood, the bright lights making it easier to find all the pieces. She was quiet for a long moment, but she'd followed him into the work area with a towel in hand, careful to remain outside the ring of glittering shards.

"You remember me," she repeated in a barely audible voice, almost like she was turning the thought over in her head.

Her tone was so…wistful, almost, that it made him look up from sweeping. She leaned a bare shoulder against one of the columns scattered throughout the room, her sinfully sexy dress clinging to a body any 1940s pinup would have envied. Something twisted in his gut.

He wanted to call it lust, but it sure as hell felt like something more.

"Definitely. You aren't exactly the kind of woman a man forgets." He wasn't happy about it, either. He couldn't help it if some of that frustration bled into his words.

She straightened from where she'd been slouching, her chin tipping higher as something defensive lit up her gaze. She folded her arms. "I am, actually. So excuse me if I found it momentarily flattering that someone like you would recall the meeting. But I can see I've disrupted your evening, Mr. Zayn." Her

Southern accent slid over his name, dragging out the vowel. "I'll get out of your hair now."

Spinning on her bare heel, she presented him with her back again. The same view that had tied him in knots the moment he entered the loft. Only this time, he was close enough to catch her. Without giving himself time to think about it, he slid an arm around her to halt her.

Immediately, he recognized the error. Knew he was crossing a professional line. He hung his head in defeat.

"I'm sorry." He sounded like he'd swallowed the broken glass. Once more, he took his hands off her with an effort, cursing his impulsiveness. Cursing himself for landing in a situation where he was alone with a woman he'd thought about too often. "You didn't ruin my evening. I should have called Marcel before barging in here tonight."

He tried to keep his eyes off the long ribbons that trailed down her back, but even when he wasn't looking at them, he was thinking about trailing them over her skin. Would it make her shiver? The mere thought of it made his body react.

She glanced back at him over her shoulder.

"You own the building, Mr. Zayn. I'm sure you don't need to call when you want to visit your own company." She scooped up a pair of jeans and a

T-shirt lying over the back of an armchair. "I'll just slip out of this dress and be on my way."

He wasn't sure what bothered him more: that he was responsible for her leaving, or that he wouldn't be the one to untie those ribbons for her tonight.

Hell.

"Don't. Go." He articulated the words carefully, keeping his tone neutral-ish. "I've interrupted you, and you're obviously doing a lot to help Marcel if you're here at this hour. If it's just the same to you, I'd much prefer you stay. Tell me what you're working on."

Slowly, she turned to face him. The anger had left her features, but she arched a skeptical brow. "You really want to know?"

She had no idea.

But now that he was here, the idea of Sable walking away from him tonight was almost painful. He knew this woman was the most talented stylist Marcel had on the payroll, so Roman couldn't afford to scare her off. But he also couldn't ignore the way she made him feel alive again after years of going through the motions of his day-to-day world. Now that he'd admitted as much, maybe he could figure out what to do about it.

"I really do." His pulse spiked at the possibilities. "And please, call me Roman."

Two

She shouldn't let the owner of the fashion label sweep the floor. But when she'd stood close to the broken glass earlier, Sable had ended up wrapped in Roman's arms as he transported her away from the mess.

Awareness of the fact that she wore nothing, nada, *zilch*, beneath the silk dress had made the contact even more intense. She was still feeling light-headed from his touch.

So she forced herself to wait patiently while Roman carried the dustpan of glass to the bin and stowed the broom. He washed his hands at the sink in the galley kitchen, the pendant lamp above the counter illuminating his high, sculpted cheekbones and the thick scruff along his square jaw. With dark eyes and dark hair that curled just above his shirt collar, he had the same Lebanese heritage that informed his brother's good looks. And yet Marcel had never lit a fire inside her. No, that special explosion to her senses was reserved for Roman.

After he dried his hands, Roman set aside the towel and flicked open the buttons on his shirt cuffs, folding the sleeves up as he spoke.

"You're very quiet for a woman who was about to tell me what you're working on." He lifted an eyebrow as he glanced her way.

Right.

No sense explaining she'd been distracted by his raw sex appeal. She'd already made enough of a fool of herself tonight. Setting aside the jeans and T-shirt she'd been ready to put back on, she crossed to the center of the room to turn off one of the spotlights.

"I'm working on some video content for the Zayn Designs social media accounts." She headed to the tripod and released her cell phone from the clamp. "The back of this dress is so unique that I thought it would be fun for viewers to see it in motion. The video just follows me as I walk away from the camera."

"May I see?" he asked, closing the distance between them to reach for her phone.

His fingers brushed hers.

She passed it to him, her body twitching with the memory of his arms around her. "Just keep in mind it's not edited."

"Of course." Gaze fixed on the screen, he tapped the play button.

Music blared from the speaker. She resisted the urge to arch up on her toes and look with him. Even though she hadn't seen the playback yet and was curious, venturing that close again seemed dangerous to her sanity.

Besides, with his attention fixed on the device, she had the chance to study him. To try to work out what it was that drew her so completely. She'd been attracted to him the first time they'd met. Tonight—once she'd recovered from being startled at his arrival—she'd been even more fascinated, experiencing a shivery awareness that wouldn't go away. And that was *before* he'd made that cryptic comment about not being able to forget a woman like her.

The remark had raised her hackles at first when she wasn't sure it had been sincere. After all, her ex had made her feel entirely forgettable. Replaceable. But after Roman's insistence she stay, she couldn't dismiss his remark. If he found her so very memorable, had he felt the same pull as she had from the very first time they'd met three months ago?

Unobserved, she allowed her gaze to rake over

him from his muscled thighs up to his narrow waist. From the flare of his back to his broad, powerful shoulders. By the time she reached his face, his dark gaze had shifted from the phone to *her*.

He was alert. Intense. And very, very aware of her attention.

"Like anything you see?" The sexy rasp of his voice skated over her skin like fingernails.

Heat bloomed in her cheeks. Pooled between her thighs.

"Whether I do or not is hardly the point," she managed, her voice a thin husk of its normal sound. Or maybe it was just difficult to hear it over the racket her heart was making, ricocheting around her rib cage like it needed a way out. "My job is too important to me to risk it with poor decisions."

"Ditto." He nodded amiably as he set her phone down on the back of a low-slung sofa. "I feel the same way about my job. Which is why I waited three months to return to New York after we met the first time."

Her breath stuck in her throat. Had she moved closer to him? They were near enough to touch. Near enough for her to wonder at the texture of the stubble along his jaw. Would it leave a mark if he rubbed his cheek over her bare skin?

Along the more sensitive flesh between her legs?

"I don't understand." She needed him to clarify.

Her senses were too high on him to make sense of words right now. "You stayed away from the studio on purpose?"

"I did." A muscle twitched in his jaw, a ripple of movement even the facial hair couldn't hide. "I told myself to respect Marcel's workspace by keeping clear of his tempting new stylist."

Would a more confident woman take that comment at face value? Sable couldn't be certain. But when *she* heard it, she had the urge to look around the room for a hidden camera and someone to reveal she'd just been punked.

Maybe some of her thoughts showed on her face because he lifted an eyebrow. "You don't believe me?"

"You run a billion-dollar company in a city famous for its beautiful people. I have no doubt there are scads of *tempting* women who throw themselves at you on a regular basis."

"Funny thing about attraction, it has to work both ways," he countered, not backing off an inch. If anything, she felt like they'd gotten closer during this exchange. "Like it is right now."

His gaze lowered to her mouth. It took a superhuman effort not to lick her lips. Her throat was as dry as dust, and she couldn't have spoken if she tried.

A small sound did escape her lips, though. A telltale, hungry whimper. His dark eyes narrowed. A growl vibrated in his chest.

His mouth hovered over hers, a breath away from kissing her. Yet not kissing her. They stood close together but not touching. And it took all her willpower not to grip his shirtfront and drag him the rest of the way to her.

"This is a bad idea." Even saying the words put her lips closer to his. Had her breathing his air.

She didn't dare look up to meet his eyes. She had the feeling she'd fall right into their dark depths.

"Probably." He didn't move away, his rough exhale fanning a loose tendril of hair that had fallen near her cheek. "That is. Unless—"

He broke off.

"Unless what?" She knew better than to grasp at straws. Didn't she? Yet her body very much craved any scenario that would end with his mouth on hers.

Was it wrong to crave his healing touch after the blow to her ego and heart she'd received today? Memories of the call from her mother still lingered. Memories that made her feel inadequate. Unwanted.

"I could leave again tomorrow," he finally continued. He clasped her chin between his thumb and forefinger, lifting it to study her face and forcing her to meet his gaze. "Stay on the West Coast for a couple of months. Try again to let things cool off."

"You're going to leave already?" She felt bereft at the thought. Rejected even.

An old pain had split open inside her. But she was sure Roman Zayn's touch could ease it. Unless he left her again.

"Tomorrow," he reiterated with new emphasis. "That way we have tonight. A window of time together where we don't have to think about work or Marcel or the consequences."

The magnitude of what he was suggesting should have daunted her. But she was too hungry for his touch. Too desperate for forgetting. More than ready for any answer that would allow her what she wanted.

"We'd be walking a fine line." The ethics were questionable. But they weren't the first people to ignore professional boundaries to indulge in hot sex.

And she knew without question it would be hot. Even now his thumb stroked the underside of her chin, stirring a deluge of longing.

"Tricky, but not impossible," he acknowledged. "It's up to you, Sable. What do you want to do?"

She knew without question he could have convinced her with a kiss long ago. He hadn't pressed that advantage, though. That he wanted her to make the call, to take ownership of what she wanted, spoke well of his intentions.

"It might be a fine line, but I have excellent balance." She lifted her hands to his chest, letting her fingers curl into the fabric of his shirt. She needed whatever he could give her tonight. "And I might die if you don't touch me soon."

Roman fused his lips to hers. Kissing. Claiming. The need to taste her had been a fire in his blood from the moment he'd stepped into the studio, so her acquiescence came not a minute too soon. She tasted like strawberries and champagne, her flavor going to his head faster than any drink.

He wrapped his arms around her and held her close, only to be reminded her dress had no back. A groan went through him at the feel of her smooth skin through the long, silky ribbons. He fought the urge to untie them and send the thin fabric to the floor in a heap. He didn't want to rush things.

"You're not wearing one damned thing under this dress." He spoke the words against her damp lips, then nipped the lower one between his teeth. "Are you?"

She sucked in a startled breath before arching her hips into his. Robbing his brain of thought. Torching any restraint he might have salvaged.

"There was no room for anything but me." She smoothed her hands down his sides and then hauled his shirttails free so she could tunnel beneath the fabric.

He ground his teeth at the feel of her nails gliding lightly over his abs, tracing the muscles, until the last of his blood rushed south.

"Don't move," he warned her, backing away to find the condom he needed. "And don't even dream about taking that dress off without me."

He spotted his bag and speared a hand into a side pocket, withdrawing what he needed before returning to her. She made one hell of a vision with her dress rumpled from his touch, her dark pile of hair slipping to one side of her head as if it would spring free of its confines at any moment. She caught her lower lip with her teeth, nibbling as she watched him.

He could swear he felt those teeth on him.

Tugging her by the hand, he led her to the suite in back, a tiny afterthought of a space with just enough square footage for a queen-size bed and nightstand. But he didn't need much room considering he wanted her all over him. Or under him. All night long.

She started to reach behind her to shut the door, but he caught her in time.

"Leave it. I need to see you." Though the lamp was off in the bedroom, the open door allowed the light from the studio to filter in.

Reaching into her hair, he found the clip that held the silky mass and undid it, watching the dark strands tumble to her shoulders.

"Good idea. I want to see you, too." She was already at work on the buttons down his shirtfront, flicking them open one after the other. Her hazel gaze followed her progress, absorbed in the sight of him. Almost as if she found him every bit as fascinating as he found her.

Impossible. Yet it felt incredibly good.

He waited until she finished, then helped her by shrugging the garment off his shoulders. There was no sound in the room save their harsh breathing and the fall of clothes to the floor, noises that only amped him up when he wanted to take his time. Savor her. Especially if he was only going to get one night.

Her gaze fell to his pants and his need surged, throbbing an urgent beat in response to the growing want in her eyes. But he wouldn't let himself get distracted from getting her out of that dress first.

"Turn around." Hands on her hips, he spun her away from him until she presented him with her back, where her hair now tangled with the long ribbons that dangled from her neck. Carefully, he gathered it to one side before pushing it forward over her shoulder.

He traced one swath of black silk with his finger, watching goose bumps rise on her skin until a shiver undulated up her spine. Satisfaction pumped through him that he could elicit a reaction from her so easily. He couldn't wait to catalog every single thing she liked. Every movement that made her breath catch and her body quiver. If he only had one night, he needed to make certain it was one she'd never forget.

Too bad he was so wound up to have her that it already took monumental effort to keep himself in check and make this about her.

Bracing himself for the feel of her against him, he slid a hand around her waist, palming the space between her hips to draw her to him. With the sweet curve of her ass pressed tight to his erection, the need to grind away the ache was fierce. Especially when she moaned at the contact, her hips doing a shimmy that had him gritting his teeth and seeing stars.

From somewhere, he gathered up enough restraint to refocus on her, the length of her lithe body visible to him over her shoulder. One ribbon still in his hand, he tugged the fabric until the front of her dress dipped low, clinging precariously to the swell of her breasts for a moment before falling to her waist. The perfect mouthfuls tipped with dusky nipples were begging for his touch. His tongue.

He licked a path down her neck while he molded the soft flesh in his hands, running his thumbs over the sensitive tips in a way that made her push back against him until they both groaned.

"I need my mouth on you." He turned her back around, the dress falling the rest of the way down her body.

He stepped over the silk and laid her on the bed,

her dark hair fanning out around her. Her breath came faster as he reached for his belt, and their eyes fastened on each other. With impatient hands he stripped off the rest of his clothes before he fell on her, keeping his weight off her with one arm while he feasted on her breasts. First one, then the other, sucking and kissing, tracing circles around the tight, pebbled peaks.

But she thwarted his plan to take his time by reaching between them to stroke him, her fingertips slowly exploring him in a way guaranteed to make him lose control if he didn't stop her. Yet the sweet tentativeness of her touch forced him to endure the sexy torment. He remembered too well the way she'd bristled when he'd talked about not being able to forget her—as if someone in her life had made her feel forgettable. Unwanted.

No way would she leave his bed without feeling thoroughly appreciated.

He kissed his way down her body, veering toward her hip before returning to her navel. Circling. Dipping. She shifted beneath him, her movements restless. Needy. He skimmed a touch down her leg before tracking back up the inside of her thigh. When she made a soft, hungry sound, he guided one leg over his shoulder and tasted her.

Her back arched, hips lifting off the bed as she offered herself to him. Roman lost himself in her, eager to feel her pleasure against his lips for the first time. He didn't have to wait long before her muscles were spasming, hips twisting. He held her steady, stroking every ounce of pleasure from her until she eased against the bed again.

By the time he lifted himself higher on the bed, he was already plotting how many ways he could take her to that brink again before the sun rose. But first, he needed to be inside her. Had to be.

She must have thought the same thing because she already had the condom packet in her hands, shaking fingers ripping open the foil. Even in the half-light from the outer room, he could see the flush in her cheeks. Color he had put there.

Possessiveness clawed at him, a feeling he hadn't experienced since—*hell*. He shut that thought down as fast as possible, then took the condom from her, a flare of anger at himself making him all the more desperate to lose himself inside her.

"Roman?"

His name on her lips gentled the self-recriminations in his head. He took a moment to roll on the protection.

"I'm right here with you," he assured her, stroking her cheek. "So ready for you."

"Can I be on top?" She sounded breathless. Excited. A little nervous?

He quieted the turmoil in his mind to tune into her. "You can have anything you want, beautiful

Sable." To prove it, he rolled to his back and hauled her on top of him; she looked like a goddess straddling his thighs. "I want to see you from every angle anyway."

Her bee-stung lips curved in a satisfied smile. He searched her eyes, making sure she was totally on board with this. But her attention was already on his body, her focus glazing with desire as she lined up her hips with his, then dragged her sex over his.

Heat blasted through him. He couldn't have held back the thrust of his hips if he tried. He gripped her waist to steady her and buried himself deep. The feel of her around him was incredible. So much better than the mindless release he'd occasionally allowed himself in the past five years.

So much better that he couldn't even dwell on the hows or whys of that. He just let the sensation build until he had to move. Had to take more.

"Sable." His grip tightened on her, fingers flexing into her softness. "I need—"

"Me, too," she gasped, wriggling on him.

Rewiring his brain so she was the center of it.

With a curse that was both pleasure and pain, he answered her movement with his own, a rhythm syncing between them that drove all thought out of his head, leaving him with nothing but burning need.

They moved as one, feasting on each other, finding out what one another liked. Which was everything. There wasn't a thing she did that didn't make him feel amazing. When he'd held off as long as he could, he reached between them to stroke her, taking her higher. He could feel when she got close, when her legs started to quake on either side of him. Only when he was sure she was there, when her body started to clamp hard around him, did he let himself go.

The release went on and on, his shout coming from the depths of his gut. When he became aware of himself again, he lowered her to her side on the bed, needing her next to him while he checked to be sure he remembered his own name.

Because, damn.

Once his breathing was somewhat back in the range of normal again, he opened an eye he hadn't realized had fallen closed. In time to see Sable bending to kiss his chest. That possessiveness he'd felt before simmered again, so he was grateful when she looked up at him through her long lashes.

"Don't go to sleep yet, Roman." She repositioned herself to tuck an elbow under her head.

He had no intention of sleeping while she was in his bed, but he didn't share that with her.

"No?" He twined a dark strand of hair around his finger, and was amazed to feel his body stir again. "What did you have in mind instead?"

"If I only have one night with you, there are

other...*things*... I want to try," she confided, her tone a sweet mixture of bold and shy that socked him in the gut.

And definitely had his body stirring now.

"Anything you want, beautiful girl." He hauled her closer to kiss her neck, savoring the brush of her breasts against his chest. "But you're going to have to be more specific."

He couldn't wait to hear what she wanted. And to deliver. But he was seriously regretting the deal he'd made with her about this lasting just one night. Already he was plotting to find a way around it without complicating things for her.

Because he would honor the pledge to leave town tomorrow. And he'd give her some time to miss him while he worked out a way to ensure that seeing her again didn't compromise her job. But once those two months were up, he had every intention of returning for more.

Three

In the eight weeks that followed her toe-curling, mind-blowing, breath-stealing night with Roman Zayn, Sable sometimes thought she must have dreamed the next-level sex with the man who owned the company she worked for.

Now, seated on the edge of the tub in the fourth-floor bathroom of her shared Brooklyn apartment, watching a second pink line appear on her pregnancy test indicator, was not one of those times.

This can't be happening.

But according to the third pregnancy test she'd taken that week, it absolutely was happening, whether she wanted to believe it or not. She just couldn't understand it. They'd used protection. Except for one time, just before dawn when they'd been half asleep and she'd straddled him before remembering the condom. Even then, it had only been a momentary error. And Sable hadn't thought twice about it because when she was with her ex-husband getting pregnant had been such a struggle.

She let her head fall against the white sink basin, wondering how and when she was going to tell Roman. He'd followed their bargain to the letter, leaving her life two months ago without a word since. While she appreciated the way he was respecting boundaries, a tiny part of her couldn't help wondering if he'd thought of her. Or if he sometimes wanted a redo of that night.

A knock sounded at the door.

"Sable?" It was Tana Blackstone, the aspiring actress who'd moved into the apartment the month before her. She was pacing in the hall outside, the volume of rock music on her phone rising and falling depending on how close she was to the door. "I'll never get this job if I go to my audition with unwashed hair."

"Coming," Sable muttered. Shoving the pregnancy test in the trash, then covering it up with a tissue for good measure since she wasn't ready to share the news, Sable stepped out into the hall.

Still wearing a sleep shirt that said Coffee, Nap, Sparkle, Repeat, Tana darted past, a guitar solo blaring from the phone in her hand. "The landlady is waiting downstairs to see you, I think," she said before shutting the door between them.

"Cybil Deschamps is here? In the house?" Sable's feet stalled on the hardwood outside her bedroom, wondering what the philanthropist cosmetics heiress could want with her.

Cybil not only owned the gorgeous brownstone that Sable now called home, but also handpicked the occupants as part of a well-publicized social experiment. The seventy-something society maven had long ago resided in the storied Barbizon Hotel, a women's residence that she credited for helping her find her footing in New York while she got her career as a model underway. Last year, Cybil had decided that pricey Big Apple real estate was making it impossible for young women to chase their dreams, and started a women's apartment of her own. As one of the city's wealthiest women, she just happened to have a Brooklyn brownstone available, and she'd offered reasonably priced rooms to talented people she deemed worthy—after a lengthy and rigorous application process, of course. Sable was grateful to her since it had been the only way she could have afforded to take the internship at Zayn Designs.

"I think so," Tana called back through the door.

"Three floors up is a long way to eavesdrop so I'm not a hundred percent sure."

Sable grabbed her bag from her bed and began the trek down to the main floor. Logically, she knew Cybil couldn't already be here to kick Sable out of the apartment, even though she suspected that having a baby while in residence would be frowned upon. Was it perhaps even in the lease's fine print? She couldn't remember but wouldn't be surprised. This gorgeous refuge overlooking Fort Greene Park was intended for single women working to get ahead in artistic careers, not accidental baby mamas faced with giving up their career ambitions to raise a child.

Her belly knotted at the thought of walking away from her career. But she wanted a baby. She'd had so much trouble getting pregnant when she'd been trying, and then there'd been the miscarriage that devastated her. While her circumstances weren't ideal for parenting right now, she would never risk this opportunity to be a mother that—for all she knew—could be her one and only chance. But she hadn't really thought about what that would mean for the dream job she'd been working so hard to get off the ground. She was on track to be a celebrity stylist, putting in extra hours to build the Zayn Designs social media accounts along with her own so that she would have a following and some contacts by the time her internship ended.

Now? She needed to rethink everything.

What would Roman say when he found out about the baby? Should she call him? Wait for him to show up again in New York? She'd been rejected by her ex for not being an effective baby-maker, so she had a lot of unresolved feelings about a partner's role in parenting. Not that Roman was anywhere close to a partner. For that matter, she wondered what Marcel would think once he learned she was pregnant with his brother's child. Would he even want her to finish the internship?

She'd almost reached the main floor—the *parlor* floor, as Cybil Deschamps called it—when she heard voices coming from the great room.

"Here she is now." Cybil's voice rang with authority across the foyer, bouncing off the twelve-foot ceilings.

Tall and blonde with perfect skin, Cybil thrived on her reputation as a charity gala queen, never missing an opportunity to network. She wore a pink-and-white vintage Chanel suit with nude pumps and a T-shirt from a recent breast cancer benefit. Beside Cybil stood a man she recognized as her son, Lucas, and a younger woman Sable had never seen before but who shared Cybil's height and Nordic good looks.

Lucas and the newcomer seemed to be studiously avoiding looking at one another, yet studying each other at the same time. Like they wanted to check each other out but didn't want to be caught.

"Hello, Cybil." Sable attempted a cheery welcome but suspected her smile was flat because her mind was still on her baby news. "I was just on my way to work. Did you need me?"

"I want to introduce you to your new housemate." She put her arm around the younger woman next to her. "This is Blair Westcott. She's not only a talented makeup artist, she's going to be working for our family business, too."

Sable thought she saw Lucas Deschamps tense at this remark, but she focused on the newcomer and extended her hand. "Sable Cordero, fourth floor. Welcome."

"Nice to meet you," Blair murmured as she shook her hand, a heavy silver charm bracelet sliding down her thin wrist. Meanwhile, Cybil went on about how much Blair and Sable could help one another with their "complementary skill sets."

"Absolutely," Sable agreed, guilt settling on her shoulders at the reminder that soon she wasn't going to be using her stylist skills anymore. Cybil would be filling her spot in the apartment in no time, and then Sable wouldn't even be around to offer the new tenant any help. "We can talk more when I get home from work, but I'm already running late."

It was true. She'd somehow lost half an hour to her

pregnancy test freak-out. Still, she felt a little twinge of guilt at the idea of leaving Blair to her own devices with Cybil, who would take up the rest of her morning with name-dropping and mapping out the younger woman's future.

Not that a map always mattered. Sable pushed open the front door to the street as she considered how far off course her own life was veering from the direction she'd envisioned.

"Good morning, Sable." It was the sexy voice from her dreams.

Roman Zayn stood at the bottom of her stoop, dressed in gray pants and a custom-fitted white shirt that she recognized as one of his brother's designs. He tugged off the aviator sunglasses.

He looked…hot, with his *GQ*-worthy style, plus a whole lot of lean muscle beneath the clothes.

"Um." She realized she was staring.

The street was quiet around them, although the park on the opposite side of DeKalb was already busy with joggers, cyclists and women pushing babies in strollers.

Babies.

The reminder made her even more tongue-tied.

"So. I picked up some coffee on my way over here." Roman nodded toward the black SUV with deeply tinted windows parked behind him. A driver sat behind the wheel. "Why don't you join me for a cup, and I can take you to work?"

She blinked and nodded, telling herself to pull it together.

Why did he have to show up now of all times? If only she could have had a couple of days to absorb the changes in her life before he came striding through her door and tilting her world all over again.

Well, she didn't have the luxury of time now.

"Sure. Thank you." She needed to figure out a way to explain to her boss she was expecting his baby despite their one-night deal.

She didn't think there was enough coffee in the city to fuel that confession.

As receptions went, Roman could have wished for better.

The woman now seated next to him in the SUV had filled his waking thoughts and starred nightly in his dreams ever since his last trip to New York. He'd royally pissed off his brother by staying away from the fashion house for so long, and Marcel was even angrier when he learned that Roman had made a brief trip to Manhattan without even staying long enough to speak with him.

Roman regretted that. But he'd taken his promise to Sable seriously. He refused to put her in a compromising professional situation, and he had been hell-bent on establishing that being with him wouldn't be a conflict of interest with her work. Because he wanted to be with her again.

No woman had gotten under his skin since his wife's death the way Sable had. And while he would never remarry or replace the only woman who would ever hold his heart, he could at least take pleasure with someone who fascinated him. Someone who seemed to enjoy their connection as thoroughly as he had.

Or so he'd thought.

But seeing Sable's reaction to him today made him second-guess what he'd remembered from their one night together. Sure, there'd been the flash of heat and awareness when their eyes met. He didn't doubt the attraction was still strong on her side, too. He'd felt it in those tense moments when they'd faced off in front of her building.

Then, she'd seemed to slip away from him. Her thoughts had gone somewhere else and he didn't have a clue how to get them back.

He watched her sip from one of the coffees he'd bought, her gaze focused on the river as they crossed the Brooklyn Bridge. Dressed in denim capris and a pink sweater that drooped off one shoulder to reveal the white lace strap of an undershirt, she looked entirely edible.

He'd been dying to taste her again for months.

"You seemed surprised to see me," he remarked finally. "Did you think I wouldn't return?"

She hit him with the full force of her hazel gaze as she put the foam cup in the molded console holder. The morning sun brought out the gold and green flecks in her eyes, subtleties he hadn't been able to appreciate in the darkened studio bedroom.

"I never doubted you'd visit the studio again, but I wasn't expecting you at my apartment." She adjusted the leather strap of her bracelet, making him wonder if he made her nervous. "I guess it makes sense that, as my employer, you'd know where I live."

"I never looked at your personnel file," he clarified. "You're easy to find in an internet search since you're living in Cybil Deschamps's apartments and they get a lot of publicity."

He hadn't realized that Sable had captured the eccentric heiress's attention through a highly competitive vetting process to award the housing situations to talented applicants.

"I couldn't have afforded to accept the internship otherwise." Her shoulder brushed against his as the vehicle turned north, and she edged back quickly. "But you probably know that, too. My hometown paper gave the story a lot of coverage."

Along with coverage of her divorce from a local would-be politician, a media angle he would have found intrusive and in poor taste even if he hadn't felt protective of her. But seeing her in an old photo with another man had been…uncomfortable, to say the least. He shouldn't feel jealous of another man in her life, but the feeling had been stark. Obvious.

His phone vibrated on the seat beside him, but he barely glanced at it, wanting to savor this time with Sable.

"They should have focused more on your accomplishments and less on your personal life." He was grateful for the gridlocked traffic; it gave them a private moment together, especially with the partition between them and the driver raised. Roman hadn't had nearly enough time to talk to her. He still needed to convince her to see him again. "Your professional track record is commendable. It was obvious why Marcel wanted you."

"Thank you. I've always wanted to be a celebrity stylist, and Marcel has given me so many opportunities to make that happen once I finish my commitment to him. I'm not even halfway through my internship, and I've already had some interest—"

She broke off suddenly, turning from him so he couldn't read her expression. Was she upset? She sounded uneasy.

"That's a good thing, isn't it?" He didn't know enough about the fashion world. The only reason he was the head of Zayn Designs was his knowledge of business and his personal capital.

He reached over the console to touch her shoulder. Encourage her gaze. When she turned back toward him, he couldn't identify the emotions in her eyes. But they swirled there.

Intensely.

"It *would* be a good thing," she started again, her voice low. "If I could take advantage of those opportunities."

She lifted her coffee for another sip while he tried to make sense of that.

"Why can't you? Are you afraid they won't still be there when you finish your year with Marcel?" He wanted to help her. To pave the way for her to use her talents. But he also didn't want to overstep.

He had to handle this relationship carefully, but being respectful of her as a professional didn't mean he shouldn't acknowledge her contributions to his business. Far from it. And if she was having problems related to the fashion house, he wanted to know about them.

The muscle beneath her right eye twitched and he wondered again if she was nervous. And it occurred to him that this conversation would be easier if she was on his lap. In his arms. Under him.

Hell. He shifted uncomfortably, beginning to think he'd underestimated her effect on him. How could he concentrate on what she was saying when he wanted her this badly?

"I can't take advantage of those opportunities, Roman." She drew in a deep breath as she met his gaze. "Because I just found out I'm pregnant."

The words he'd never expected to hear left a phantom echo in the silence.

They circled in his head. Blanked his brain of everything else. He had questions but didn't trust himself to ask them in a way that would be appropriate. Hell, he didn't have the brainpower to determine what *was* appropriate. Knowing that, he waited. Watching her. Hoping if she spoke again maybe he could make sense of the pronouncement.

Licking her lips, she continued. "I only just found out for certain, so I'm still trying to wrap my brain around what it means. But you're the only man I've been with in the last year, so even though we took the right precautions. Well, mostly…"

Her words trailed off.

She didn't need to finish the sentence, though, because he recalled that last time they'd been together when they hadn't been careful enough.

"I remember," he acknowledged, knowing he wasn't doing enough to take responsibility. To support her. "It never occurred to me to follow up with you about that—"

With a hand on his arm, she halted his words. It was the first contact she'd initiated.

"That wasn't on you," she said, shaking her head

as her hand fell away again, retreating toward her coffee cup. When she spoke again, her voice was quieter. "I didn't think twice about it at the time because I had trouble getting pregnant when I was trying."

The unexpected admission—and the hint of old hurt it revealed—felt like the most intimate thing he'd learned about her so far. Oddly, that small glimpse of vulnerability finally nudged his brain into gear.

Later, he'd think about the repercussions of this. Figure out what it meant for him and for his future. Right now, it was imperative to solidify some trust with Sable. Ensure she wouldn't cut ties with him or Zayn Designs to return to Louisiana and her family. If she was carrying his child, he needed her here.

"I'm sorry the timing isn't ideal for you, Sable." He shifted toward her in his seat to look her full in the face. Then, wanting to emphasize what he said next, he took both her hands in his and squeezed. "But I'm here now, and I can help. I'll support you in whatever comes next."

He meant it, too. But he also knew, underneath that offer of support, there lurked a sharp ache that he had missed out on this with his wife. He scrubbed a hand over his face to give himself time to school his expression.

Annette had wanted so badly to be a mother. And while Roman planned to keep his most personal vow to her, grief knotted in his chest that he would be sharing this with another woman. He felt disloyal.

"I'm keeping this baby," Sable told him emphatically as the SUV rolled to a stop outside the Zayn Designs building. A defensive note lurked in her voice. "That's my next step, Roman. I'm going to make a doctor's appointment and do everything in my power to have a healthy pregnancy. I won't ask you to be a part of the baby's life if you would rather not, but I *will* see this through."

"Good." Relieved, he felt some of the knot in his chest ease. He couldn't afford for Sable to misread his tension. He squeezed her hands again to indicate to her they wanted the same thing. "I'm glad. And rest assured, I will also see this through. I'd never abandon my child. I hope you'll allow me to attend the doctor's appointment with you."

Her lips parted in an O of surprise; clearly, she hadn't been expecting that. But something softened in her expression, and the wariness faded in her hazel eyes, giving him hope that his declaration wasn't unwelcome.

"Of course." She tugged her hands free to retrieve the leather handbag on the seat beside her. "I'll text you once I set it up." She moved to get out of the vehicle, then turned to look at him over her shoulder. "Aren't you coming upstairs?"

"Not yet." Mostly because the baby news had

thrown him for a loop. He wasn't ready to conduct business as usual with his brother right now. He also had a lot of planning to do, beginning with securing a place to stay in New York now that he'd be spending more time here. "I've got a couple of other appointments this morning, but I'll connect with Marcel later today."

He passed her the coffee cup after she stepped onto the sidewalk.

"Oh. Well, thanks for the ride, then." She nibbled her lip for a moment, drawing his attention to her delectable mouth. "And can we keep this news to ourselves for a little while? Just until we've had some time to get more comfortable with it?" She drew her jacket tighter around herself, the movement drawing his attention to her narrow waist. The curve of her hips.

And damn, but he wanted the right to touch her again. Taste her. But he couldn't risk pressing her right now. She was too jittery.

"That's fine," he agreed, even though he hadn't thought that far ahead. "We'll talk more soon, and I hope to hear from you later about that appointment."

She gave him a nod before turning to enter the building. Roman watched her leave, then used the call button to let the driver know their next destination. He had a lot to accomplish today, but one good thing about the baby news was that he wouldn't have to talk Sable into spending time with him again.

With the doctor's appointment coming up, he didn't have to. One way or the other, he'd be seeing her soon. He just hoped by then she would be open to his next proposition. Because if she was already pregnant, he couldn't imagine a single reason they couldn't indulge in many more heated nights together.

Four

Sable battled her dread of doctors' offices and showed up at the obstetrician's early the next week. She'd texted Roman the details of the visit the same day she'd dropped the baby bombshell on him, and he'd replied that he'd be there. Outside of that communication, she'd only seen him briefly one other time at the studio and they hadn't spoken. He'd texted her a few times, however, checking in to see how she felt. Asking if she needed anything.

That had been…nice. In fact, she appreciated the space to get her head together as much as the reminders that he was willing to be a presence in her life. Well, the baby's life. She had no illusions about where his loyalties lay given that they barely knew one another.

"Sable Cordero?" A nurse dressed in pink scrubs and carrying a clipboard waved her into an exam room for the ultrasound.

Still no Roman.

She blinked away the hurt she shouldn't be feeling. So what if he'd only been paying lip service to wanting to be a part of this pregnancy? She planned to move forward with or without him, so not having him beside her today shouldn't upset her so much.

It was just that she had hoped Roman would distract her from how nervous she was about being here, and how it reminded her of all the other times she'd wound up at her physician's office in Baton Rouge. Or later when she'd visited the fertility clinic. The memories brought a thorny sense of failure and shame she'd scarcely admitted to herself, let alone shared with anyone. Those emotions were too personal, too negative. What was worse was that she didn't even feel *entitled* to them after having met women who'd struggled with infertility far longer than she had.

When the nurse left, Sable dove for her handbag to find her phone in an effort to distract herself. She'd find a social media feed full of puppies, maybe. Or cats in costume. That was always good for a smile. She had just unlocked the screen to see two missed messages when she heard a commotion outside in the lobby.

And was that Roman's voice?

A knock sounded at the exam room door and the nurse poked her head in.

"Ms. Cordero? There's a gentleman here for you—" She didn't finish speaking before Roman appeared behind her.

Sable felt a spark of awareness at the sight of him. His hair was messy, like he'd tugged on it a few times. His cheeks were flushed, his expression agitated.

"He can come in." Sable cursed her sudden breathlessness at the sight of him, her voice sounding all wrong.

Still clutching her phone, she wrapped her arms around herself, feeling suddenly self-conscious in the thin exam gown.

"Sorry I'm late." Roman strode in, his dark eyes sweeping over her as the nurse let the door fall closed behind them. His presence seemed to fill the room, making it feel smaller than it had just a moment ago. "There was an accident on the West Side Highway. I tried to call."

"I've had my phone off," she explained. Remembering that she was still holding it, she slipped the device back into her handbag. "I'm one of those overly compliant types that actually follow through on shutting it down at a doctor's office." She should have thought to check for messages instead of assuming the worst. But then, she'd grown used to doing baby-related doctor visits on her own, so maybe she'd been expecting Roman to bail on her.

The tension in Roman's shoulders eased a fraction at her admission, and the corners of his lips lifted in a smile. "So the temptress of my fantasies is a rule follower at heart?"

"If you mean me, um…yes. Too much so," she admitted, trying to ignore the warmth in her cheeks. She'd been so consumed with worries about making responsible decisions for a baby's future that she hadn't thought as much about that night with Roman. Let alone if he might want a repeat. "And the ultrasound technician should arrive soon to listen for the heartbeat. All you missed were paperwork and blood work."

He jammed his fists in the pockets of his tailored black pants. "I missed being here with you. My goal was to support what you're going through, not to waltz in for the fun part."

Sable was saved from picking through all the ways that statement appealed to her by another knock at the exam room door. The ultrasound technician entered and introduced herself as Melissa. The tall, stately woman was shadowed by Pink Scrubs, who helped Sable get comfortable on the exam table before disappearing again.

The flurry of movement around her made what was happening become more real. More exciting and scary at the same time. Sable took deep breaths and hoped for the best. Her blood work had confirmed a pregnancy, so at ten weeks, they ought to hear a heartbeat. She'd confided her concerns about her miscarriage earlier, prompting the doctor's decision to go ahead with an ultrasound even though the practice usually waited until after the eleventh week.

Strictly a precaution, the doctor had said, adding that it would give Sable peace of mind. The woman hadn't recommended she curtail any activities, insisting she'd done a thorough review of Sable's health history and saw no indication that her previous miscarriage would be a cause for concern. Still, some of her worry must have shown on Sable's face because Roman laid a hand on her shoulder.

"Are you ready?" His focus remained trained on her face while the tech prepared the wand.

Unable to restrain herself, she gripped Roman's wrist and held tight, grateful he was here. That he cared what happened. Blinking through the onslaught of emotions, she nodded up at him.

"Ready."

Two things stood out to Roman as the tech wielded the wand on Sable's flat belly like she was conducting an orchestra.

First, the gorgeous woman on the exam table in front of him was carrying his child, and the start to this pregnancy was healthy and perfect in every way. He heard it for himself in the strong heartbeat. He understood it in the reassuring way the tech kept pointing out all the normal markers of a ten-week pregnancy.

That part was nothing short of awe-inspiring.

But the other thing that Roman couldn't help noticing during the ultrasound was that Sable was scared.

His first clue had been her death grip on his hand, making him all the more pissed at himself for not being there on time to get a better read on her. What had her so worried? Granted, there were a million possible answers to that question since she hadn't been expecting to get pregnant while trying to establish herself in a competitive industry. No doubt she had a lot on her mind with all the changes ahead. But since his one and only role in this baby business prior to the birth was to make sure Sable was safe and happy, he couldn't help feeling he was already failing.

Which was simply unacceptable.

Ten minutes later, with Sable dressed in a leopard-print trench coat she wore open over a white shirt-dress and ankle boots, they took the elevator down to street level in silence while Roman strategized his best approach. He needed to spend more time with her, figure out what was bothering her, and fix it. The sooner she started trusting him, the better for the sake of shared childcare. And if they ended up working out some of this attraction that had him on edge whenever he was around her, so much the better.

But first things first. He'd already texted their driver to meet them out front.

"You look great," Roman told her as their shoulders brushed inside the elevator cabin. He hoped to transition from the easy compliment into touchier subjects. He skimmed his fingers over her sleeve strap, feeling an answering shiver through her. "Is that one of Marcel's designs?"

She laughed; it was the first smile he'd seen from her since he'd returned to New York. "I can't afford your brother's clothes. But thank you. I have fun putting outfits together. The coat was a good vintage find."

The elevator settled on ground level with an unsteady jerk that had his arm wrapping around her. The possessiveness he'd felt that first night with her had only intensified since learning she carried their baby.

"It's not just the clothes." He released her as they headed toward the exit so he could hold the door for her. "You have the pregnancy glow working for you today. Have you been feeling well?"

He resented missing the first half of her appointment since he'd lost the chance to hear her talk about her health. He wanted to know how she was sleeping, if she was eating enough.

"A little more tired than usual, but I've heard that's normal." Her words mingled with the screech of a fire engine's siren as it careened past.

"Should you ask Marcel about modifying your schedule?" He'd agreed to keep the news between them for now, but he needed for his brother to be understanding about her condition.

"Not yet." Eyes wary, she hesitated outside the SUV when he opened the rear door of the vehicle. "I worked so hard to land this job, Roman. As long as the doctor says I'm okay to continue, I will. And I was going to hit some consignment shops in this area while I was up this way."

Meaning he wasn't going to have a chance to find out why she'd been scared in the doctor's office, let alone fix it.

"You need lunch," he urged, thinking of her health. "I thought we could share a bite and talk more about what's ahead."

"I have a whole list of items I need to find for a photo shoot." She withdrew a scrap of paper from her pocket, still making no move to enter the vehicle. "One of the stores is just around the corner."

"Dinner then," he suggested, but was unwilling to

push her. He didn't want to add to her worries, but the thought of not seeing her for another week was like a vise constricting his chest. "We deserve to celebrate, Sable. Hearing that heartbeat was pretty incredible."

"Yeah, it was." A gravity in her hazel eyes told him how much that moment had meant to her, too. She dropped her list back into her pocket.

It still blew him away that he was going to share this monumental thing with her when they'd spent so little time together. He couldn't afford to screw it up.

"It's not like I can celebrate with anyone else," he reminded her. "Since we're keeping it just between us."

Finally, she nodded. "I should be done with the photo shoot by seven if you want to meet afterward."

The stranglehold on his chest eased. "Should I pick you up at the studio?"

"That would be great." Her lips curved slightly. Not a real smile like he'd glimpsed before, but at least he was grateful that he'd have more time with her tonight.

They could get on the same page about the future and what this baby meant for them. As long as he could keep the feelings he had about the pregnancy separate from the red-hot attraction he still felt toward Sable, he'd be fine. He could indulge the latter without threatening the vow he'd made to stay true to his wife's memory.

One day at a time. It was the only way he knew how to move forward after life had stolen everything precious to him.

"Great work today, Sable." Marcel Zayn stood in front of an antique mirror near the loft's elevator, putting on a dinner jacket. "I hope you snapped some images for your look book. I already posted a few candids on the Instagram page. The clothes and concept really worked well together."

Sable hugged the praise close to her chest as she put the last few sample garments back on the rolling rack. A new digital magazine had done a focus piece on Zayn Designs, and Marcel had okayed a photo shoot of their own to overlap the time the reporter was on site so they had some control over the images that would run with the story. They worked hard to leverage as much content as possible out of opportunities like today's, and Sable appreciated the designer's generosity in giving her credit.

"Thank you. We lucked out with the models. They really got on board with it." Sable had suggested a few poses, and the models had been so comfortable with each another. Their chemistry had resulted in a great shot of the male model untying the ribbons on the back of the woman's dress.

No mystery where she'd gotten *the* idea for *that*

sexy sequence of shots. She probably owed Roman a creative credit.

Marcel laughed as he tugged his shirtsleeves to the perfect length underneath the jacket. "You think? There were sparks flying all over the place. It was so damned steamy to watch I ended up calling Parker for a second date." His phone chimed in his pocket while he was refastening a French cuff. "That's probably him now."

He stepped onto the elevator when it arrived. Sable watched him, noticing the resemblance between the designer and Roman in the way they moved with athleticism and grace.

"Night, Marcel." She was relieved Roman hadn't crossed paths with his brother since it was almost seven now. She'd asked Roman to keep the baby news quiet, but she wasn't sure where they stood in regard to letting other people know they occasionally…dated?

Hooked up?

Hell, *she* didn't know where they stood with one another, so no wonder she wasn't sure how to explain it to anyone else. Add to that the taboo factor of an intern dating the CEO, and she really wasn't ready to draw attention to it.

That was one of many reasons she'd been wary about spending more time with him. It was not like the attraction had dimmed since they'd torn off their clothes and feasted on each other all night long. Even today during her appointment, when she'd been stressed and anxious, she'd felt the tug of awareness for him. What would it be like tonight when they were alone over dinner?

Especially now, with the memories of that sexy photo shoot that had her reliving every second she'd spent in this studio with Roman ten weeks ago? She'd basically memorialized it by having the models reenact the encounter—up until the clothes came off, of course—in the photoshoot today. She allowed her fingers to walk from one hanger to the next on the rolling rack in the quiet studio, lingering on the dress she'd worn that night with Roman.

How would she put those thoughts out of her mind once she met Roman tonight? Her focus needed to be on the practical matter of sharing parenting duties, not remembering all the ways he could take her to extraordinary sensual heights. She couldn't afford to lose focus on what was most important.

Not with a baby at stake.

The thought had her returning to her bag and taking out the printed ultrasound image from the doctor's office. Studying the profile of her baby's face had her spine straightening, her shoulders braced for the weight of the world. Because she'd take it all on for the sake of that heartbeat she'd heard today. So strong and fierce.

The memory was precious, the moment unforgettable. And it was made all the more so by the fact that the man beside her had seemed as blown away by it as she'd been. Roman had gripped her hand tightly when the sound of the heartbeat had filled the exam room. She'd glimpsed his face, and there'd been a moment of raw emotion there. Deep. Complex. Hope and awe, but perhaps tinged with a hint of regret?

She'd looked away fast, feeling like she'd seen something overly private. Personal. He'd made it clear afterward he'd viewed the strong heartbeat as a reason to celebrate, but she couldn't shake the sense that there was more to it than that for Roman.

Still, whatever he felt about her pregnancy, at least he'd been there with her. That was more than she could say about her ex-husband, whose work had always trumped the doctor appointments he viewed as Sable's responsibility. She respected Roman's desire to be there. Admired it. And yes, she'd been glad to share something momentous with the only other person who had as much connection to this tiny life as she did.

A moment later, the elevator doors reopened with a soft swish and she slid the ultrasound photo back into her bag.

Even before she saw Roman, her body hummed with the sensation of being watched, her skin tingling and the hair at the back of her neck lifting.

"Sable." His voice rubbed over her like a touch, the low tone giving her goose bumps.

She wished she could write off the reaction as pregnancy hormones, but it had been the same exact way as that night they'd spent together. Right here, in this same spot.

Memories crowded her as he drew closer. He'd changed clothes since the appointment. His hair was still damp around the collar of a black button-down as if he'd just showered. The gray pants he wore had a subtle weave, and his loafers were casual. He looked good enough to eat. She wanted to drift closer, guessing he smelled even better.

But she had her priorities straight now, and she wasn't going to waver on them.

"Hi." She reached for her coat, which was hanging on one of the rolling racks of the clothes she'd used for the photo shoot. "You didn't have to come up. I could have met you downstairs."

He was instantly at her side, taking over the task of settling her coat on her shoulders, sliding her hair out from under the collar so that it fanned out over her back.

"From now on, whatever I can do to make your life easier, Sable, I will." He turned her around, and she was suddenly facing him while he wrapped one side of her coat over the other before tying the belt at her waist. "Get used to it."

The gesture was both intimate and sweet, accelerating her pulse and making her feel cared for at the same time. And, just as she'd suspected, the scent of him—like woodsmoke and pine—only made her want to lean into him.

"Where are we going?" She retrieved her bag, moving away from him to collect herself.

"It's a surprise." He returned to the elevator and pressed the button, then lingered by the rolling rack where the clothes from the shoot were lined up on hangers.

With an unerring eye, he zeroed in on the dress she'd worn the night they'd been together. While he waited for her to shut down the lights, he slid his thumb and forefinger over one long ribbon. The hanger swayed gently in the wake of the movement.

Sable was pretty sure she did, too.

The elevator doors slid open.

"Ready?" he asked, turning dark eyes on her when she hesitated.

Was she ready for more time with this charismatic man who turned her inside out? She should be resisting him. But for practical purposes, she had to plan a way forward with Roman so they could raise a child together. She could ignore her hormones for a couple of hours to engage in what amounted to a business dinner, couldn't she?

It wouldn't be easy. But she owned her choices, and she would be the mother her baby deserved.

"I am." Reaching his side, she stepped into the elevator. "Let's go."

Five

"How are you feeling?" Roman asked Sable on the short drive from his brother's studio to their dinner destination.

He'd told himself that it was just as well that she'd declined his lunch invitation since it had given him more time to work on his game plan with the woman seated next to him. After her ultrasound, he'd been both elated and gutted at the reality of becoming a father, and he ran the risk of letting too much slip in front of Sable. He wasn't going to begin their co-parenting relationship while she thought he wasn't fully on board with raising a child.

Now he'd had time to lock down that unruly knot of reactions so he could make this evening 100 percent about her.

"I'm not as tired today as I have been the last couple of weeks, so that's a win." She gave him a small smile, her dark hair trailing over one shoulder. She'd tied it with what looked like a fabric swatch, the ends of the red velvet unfinished and fraying.

"No morning sickness?" He still resented that he'd been late for her appointment and hadn't heard the full dialogue with the physician.

"None so far." She sounded relieved about that as the vehicle rolled to a stop in front of the Madison Square Park Tower. She glanced up and down the street around the granite base of the soaring sculptural glass building. "We're eating here?"

"I ordered in for us in case you wanted to put your feet up," he explained. "I know you had a busy day preparing for the photo shoot, so I had the concierge coordinate a restaurant delivery. Although it's not too late to do something else if you prefer."

"No. That sounds great, actually." She picked up her purse while he exited the vehicle.

After helping her down, he released his hold on her hand, wanting her to be at ease. If he had his way, he would have been touching her every second since he'd set foot in the design studio, but this wasn't about him. He needed her to feel comfortable with him.

"Did you find everything you needed for the shoot?" he asked as he led her past the door attendant and into the elevator that would take them to the fiftieth floor.

"I found all I wanted and then some." Her soft drawl lingered over the words like a caress, a smile teasing around her lips. "Marcel was really pleased with how it all came together and we got a lot of great images."

"Are they posted on the social media accounts yet?" He pulled his phone from his pocket. "I checked about an hour ago, but I didn't see an update."

"You did?" She sounded surprised. "I mean, it makes sense you'd follow the account. I just didn't know how much of your professional time was devoted to the design house since you've only been in the studio a couple of times."

He paused in the middle of scrolling to meet her gaze. "That was in deference to you, Sable. I was trying not to make you uncomfortable with how much I wanted—how much I still want—you."

She swallowed, her legs shifting beneath her dress in a way that sent a growl up the back of his throat. He only just barely managed to suppress it, but he did because that was not what this night was about.

Even if pregnancy had made her all the more irresistible, with deeper color in her cheeks and added curve to her breasts. He'd noticed the changes earlier at the doctor's office. He wondered what other subtle things he would notice about her body if he had the chance to explore it more thoroughly.

The elevator door opened on his floor, providing a much-needed distraction from the temperature spike between them. Still clutching his phone, he gestured the way to his door and let her in.

"And, to your point," he added, hoping to pick up the thread of their conversation before he mentally undressed her anymore. "I spend about one quarter of my time on Zayn Designs, running the business side so Marcel can concentrate on what he does best."

He took her coat from her, careful not to linger over the body he wanted to touch so badly. Sable seemed to be on the same page since she quickly darted away to check out the view through the floor-to-ceiling windows in the living room while he turned his attention to the catering bags on the marble kitchen counter.

"Your place is really nice," she observed softly, her white shirtdress reflecting a blue glow from lights near the clock tower visible at 1 Madison Avenue. "Did you just move in? I remember you were staying at the studio last time you were in town."

He ground his teeth at the reminder of the only

time they'd shared a bed. "Our father owns this apartment. He was in Manhattan at the same time as me two months ago, so I chose not to stay here. But he doesn't use this space often. He and my mother are in London for the next six weeks, so there's no chance we'll run into them here." He withdrew a platter from the warming drawer beneath the oven and carried it to the dining table that bridged the kitchen and living room in the open-concept layout. "But I've already looked at a few other places around town since I'll need something of my own."

"You're moving to New York?" she asked quickly, clearing away a pewter bowl that was a centerpiece on the table, making room for the food he carried.

Was it his imagination or was there a hint of panic in her voice?

"Not full-time." He kept his answer casual, returning to the kitchen to bring in the catering bags, plates and silverware. "Zayn Equity is based on the West Coast, so I'll maintain a presence in Los Angeles. But you're in New York, and so is my firstborn, so it makes sense to maintain a home base here."

She turned away to retrieve the two glasses he'd left on the kitchen counter, and her face was momentarily hidden. When she returned, her gaze was trained on the table, prompting him to check in with her.

"I hope that's not a problem," he said, taking the

glasses from her and setting them on the table. It was killing him not to just wrap her in his arms and offer her the undeniable physical connection they shared. But since he knew they couldn't solve their deeper problems that way, he withdrew her chair for her instead.

"No. Of course not." She took the seat he offered. "I'm just not sure that I can afford to stay in New York once the baby arrives. Even if I can find work here, I'll need to move out of my current apartment since it's intended for women launching careers in creative fields, not working mothers."

He took that in—along with the obvious tension she felt about the situation—and hoped to distract her with the meal before resuming the topic. These were issues he knew damn well he could solve if she'd allow him. For now, he pulled out the containers from the catering bags and poured two glasses of water from a chilled bottle.

"Dig in," he urged as he took the seat across from her. "I didn't know what you'd be in the mood for, and I wanted to be sure there was something you'd like, so I ordered a little of everything."

"Oh, wow," she murmured as she raised the silver lid on one of the dishes, revealing an assortment of pastas. "This looks delicious."

"And I've got some chicken options over here." He lifted the lid on the dish closer to him to show her.

"The bread is in there." He unwrapped a tea towel from a basket, then began to fill his own plate. "Do you mind telling me what you had planned for work after the internship if you hadn't gotten pregnant?"

"I counted on Marcel's connections to keep me working as a stylist in New York for at least another year or two so I could build my network and my reputation." She slid some fettuccine, chicken and tomato slices onto her plate as she spoke, and it pleased him inordinately to see her eat. To know he'd fulfilled a need for her when she was carrying his child. It made him all the more certain he wanted to do more. "After that, I would have tried to make the leap to working in Hollywood, dressing celebrities."

"So don't leave New York for the baby's sake if you'll want to resume working here eventually. Take a sabbatical to give birth and see how you feel. Come back in a year when you're ready, and you'll be able to pick up where you left off."

She laughed. "Spoken like a man. A wealthy man, at that."

"Is that so?" He wasn't accustomed to his input being dismissed.

Perhaps his frustration came through in his voice because she straightened in her chair and met his gaze.

"Yes. Because I'm not asking you to solve my problems for me. And even if I had solicited your advice, there are subtleties you're not taking into account."

"So let's talk through them." He pushed the bread-basket closer to her, wondering how he could convince her to let him help. "Figure out a plan."

"Okay. First of all, it would be difficult enough to finance a year off even if I return to Baton Rouge. But I'd never be able to afford it in New York." She paused to take a sip of her water, and he noticed how the skyline behind her had turned fully dark through the wall of windows. "Furthermore, my life will change radically once a baby arrives. I'm not sure I'll even continue chasing my professional dream once my priorities shift to accommodate a child."

Her words tugged at a memory, an old conversation with Annette about having a family and what it would mean to her. How she wanted to stay at home to finger-paint and run the sprinkler in the backyard so their kids could play in it on hot afternoons. She'd been so certain of what kind of mom she wanted to be that she'd made Roman able to envision it, too.

That sting of disloyalty jabbed him again, but he forced himself to ignore it to focus on Sable.

"You're right." His jaw felt stiff when he spoke, making him realize he'd been grinding his teeth, gnawing on the past. "You deserve more time to figure out what works best for you. Why don't I look for a bigger space so you can move in with me for a year?"

* * *

This was all moving too fast.

Sable didn't want to appear ungrateful for Roman's generosity, but she absolutely couldn't allow him to step into a role where she could grow dependent on him. Jack had been her husband and she couldn't count on him. She sure as hell couldn't trust that Roman Zayn, her too-sexy boss with no legal tie to her at all, would follow through on what he proposed.

Better to remain independent.

"I can't do that." She twirled her fork through the fettucine noodles. "And I need more time before I make any big decisions about what's next."

"But you don't want to be in the middle of the move when you're eight months pregnant. Wouldn't it be best to relocate somewhere else soon, so you have time to get settled without exhausting yourself?"

It was a valid point. And yet…

"Could we revisit that in a couple of weeks?" She was stressed enough about the pregnancy without heaping more decisions on top of it. "After I get through the first trimester?"

He frowned. "Do you have any reason to…be concerned?"

She let out a sigh, knowing he deserved the truth, but still hating to dredge up the hurt.

"I told you that I had trouble getting pregnant,"

she began softly, taking a roll from the basket and buttering it. "But I didn't tell you that I also had a miscarriage."

His fork clattered onto his plate, and the next thing she knew his arm was around her, his chair drawn close to hers so he could give her the comfort of… him.

"I'm sorry, Sable." He spoke into her hair, his lips pressing close to her temple.

Touched at his kindness and understanding, she set aside her bread and allowed herself a moment to turn to him, her forehead tucking into the crook of his neck to absorb his strength. His empathy.

Had Jack ever held her like this when she'd needed desperately to be comforted? Her eyes burned as she realized how much she'd needed that, and how Roman offered it so completely.

"Thank you." With an effort, she picked her head up and tried to resume their conversation.

Except then they were just a breath apart, with his arm still a warm weight around her shoulders. His jaw was close enough for her to kiss. Taste. Bite.

She closed her eyes to dial down the temptation.

His hand shifted slightly to palm the middle of her back.

"How far along were you?" He cupped her face in his other hand, tipping her chin up.

She opened her eyes and met his dark scrutiny.

In that moment, she was grateful for the physical attraction. The raw tug of it kept her from falling into unhappy memories.

"Twelve weeks." How long had it been since she'd shared the story? "I started bleeding the day before my first ultrasound appointment. I felt so relieved when I hit that twelve-week mark, too. But then..."

She winced at the memory. She placed her hand over the spot, as if she could ward off the old hurt and protect the new life there now.

"I can't imagine how tough that must have been for you." His fingers sifted through the ends of her hair, smoothing some of the strands that hung down her back. His other hand fell away from her cheek to cover hers where it rested on her lap.

The tenderness of the touch made her breath catch.

"I fell into a dark place afterward." She hadn't been able to pull herself out of the sadness, so she'd scheduled an appointment with a counselor. Which had been a blessing because she'd needed the support all the more when Jack checked out on her. "Then my husband served me with divorce papers two weeks later."

"Bastard."

She knew Jack had tired of putting so much effort into what he thought should be easy, but she hadn't realized until he left her how expendable she'd been.

"That about sums it up," she agreed. "In the end, the miscarriage hurt more than the dissolution of my marriage. It took some time before I was able to focus on myself again. Getting this job with Marcel was the best possible affirmation that I'd made the right choice to return to my dreams."

"All the more reason not to turn your back on it now." Letting go of her, Roman moved his plate closer so they could finish their meal side by side.

She missed his touch, even if she understood his need to reestablish boundaries. Or at least, she thought that was what he was doing. Apparently he had more discipline about their attraction than she did if he could stay away for two months. She might have asked for space this most recent time, but she'd regretted it a week later.

Even now, with the stress of an unexpected pregnancy and her total commitment to making good choices for her baby, she still craved Roman's kiss. His hands on her. She blinked through the haze of longing to consider his words.

"I understand why you think so. But I feel like I can't make any long-term decisions until I pass that twelve-week mark." She recrossed her legs under the table, grazing his calf in a way that she would have sworn was accidental.

Yet she couldn't deny she enjoyed the way his grip tightened on his fork and his body tensed.

"What did the obstetrician say about the miscarriage?" he asked after a moment. "Did she think you were at greater risk this time?"

"No. She reviewed my medical records before the appointment, and said everything was okay. She cleared me for…normal activity." She felt heat crawl up her face at the memory of that conversation.

Finished with her meal, she pushed the plate aside and took a drink of her water to drown some of the fire inside.

"You asked her about sex specifically?" His voice dropped to a deeper tone, pinpointing exactly the topic that had made her skin warm.

"I did." She suppressed a shiver, then forced herself to meet his gaze.

The answering heat she saw in his brown eyes sent her pulse into overdrive.

"Good." He gave a nod of satisfaction. "That's… good."

For a moment, she was mesmerized by the memory of what this man could do to her with a simple kiss. But then he shoved away from the table to clear their plates.

Right.

Because they were here to work out logistics for sharing a child. Or at least talk through what the next few weeks would look like. She'd told herself that this would be a business dinner, but she was already contemplating being in his arms again.

Or wrapping her legs around his hips.

She got up and began to help him, carrying the food back to the ultramodern kitchen. Clearly she needed something to keep her hands busy so she didn't wind up putting them all over Roman.

"I've got this, Sable." He took the dishes from her as she rounded the gray-and-white granite countertop. "'Normal activity' for you doesn't include cleanup when I'm around."

She didn't argue. Because how nice was that? Instead, she took a seat on the white leather barstool overlooking the kitchen as he worked. He wrapped the leftovers and stowed them in the refrigerator before pulling out a bottle of sparkling water and a container of raspberries. Then, finding two champagne flutes, he rinsed off a few berries to drop into the bottom of each glass before pouring the sparkling water over them.

"We're celebrating tonight," he reminded her, sliding a glass along the granite toward her. "Hearing that heartbeat today blew me away. So I'm going to propose a toast to our healthy baby."

He stood beside the barstool, his arm draped over the back of the leather seat. He was close, but not touching her.

"I'll drink to that." She lifted her glass, touched at his thoughtfulness. "Cheers."

He tipped his flute to hers, and their glasses tinkled softly.

She watched the bubbles climbing the inside of the cut crystal glass, the column of his throat working as he took a drink.

For a moment, he seemed to sense her perusal because he set his glass aside and returned her steady look, causing her pulse to pick up speed.

"Now that I understand why you want to wait to make plans for the baby," he began, settling a hand on top of hers, "I'll try not to pressure you about moving in with me, at least for the next two weeks. But I'm going to continue to look for a place in New York so that it's ready if we need it. At the very least, I want to be here for the pregnancy and the remaining appointments."

She wanted to argue that it wasn't necessary. That she couldn't possibly move in with him since she wouldn't allow herself to rely on him that way. She needed to remain in control of her life and her future, even if that meant returning home to raise her baby in Baton Rouge.

Still, she appreciated his support. And she'd never forget the way he'd held her when she told him about the miscarriage. That moment…said a lot about him.

"Thank you," she finally managed, though she

had to look away so as not to betray the confused tangle of feelings.

Then Roman, perhaps wanting to change the subject out of empathy for her, reached for his cell phone on the counter.

"I never had a chance to look at the photos from today," he explained, tapping the screen to life before scrolling.

All at once, the memory of the photo shoot returned. And in particular, the sexy vignettes she'd recreated from her night with Roman.

"Oh. Um." She wasn't sure exactly what had been posted online, so maybe the images weren't anything that Roman would link to her night with him. "I forgot about that."

She reached across the counter for the sparkling water bottle and refilled their glasses. Was it because she'd need to cool down after seeing the images? Or to hide her nervousness over whether Roman would recognize how she'd created her own visual ode to their time together?

Probably both.

She was already pouring the second glass when he made a strangled sound. Spilling a little water on the counter, she set the bottle aside to peer past where his strong arm was propped on the granite.

There, on the screen, a dark-haired model glanced over her shoulder toward a man only visible from behind. He was shirtless. She presented her back to him, two long ribbons framing her spine, and the man was tugging one free.

The shot was sizzling hot but didn't come close to capturing what those same moments had felt like when she'd lived them out with Roman two months ago. Blindly, she reached for the champagne flute, wishing she could stand under a cold shower of that raspberry-flavored water.

"Holy hell," Roman growled, his jaw flexing. His shoulder tensed. And his body heat became like a furnace beside her.

"Agreed." She slid his refilled glass toward him while she downed the contents of hers. "Although, in my defense, your brother urged me to do something sexier this time. So I couldn't help that this came to mind."

Straightening slowly from where he'd been leaning on the counter, Roman turned on her. He reached for her stool and spun it by the armrests so that she faced him fully. Then, arms bracketing her, he leaned closer.

"I did my best to give you space." His voice sounded gravelly.

"Thank you." She nodded, her heartbeat kicking hard inside her chest. "I know you have."

The leather upholstery creaked in his hard grip. He stepped between her knees, no quarter given because she was wearing a dress. The hem crept higher on her thighs. His gaze burned a hole through her.

"It's not easy to be impartial when I know you're thinking about that night as much as I am." His breath stirred her hair as he spoke close to her ear.

"I'm sure it isn't," she murmured, unable to argue with him when he could see the proof of her thoughts right there in those photos.

An ache of desire twisted low in her belly. She shifted in her seat, her knee brushing his leg and sending a bolt of awareness through her. A whimper escaped her throat before she could swallow it back.

And then, after a scowl and a curse, Roman's lips covered hers.

Six

All evening long, Roman had done his damnedest to hold back. He'd had a game plan for putting her at ease. For ensuring she understood he wanted more than just sex. He wanted to be a part of his child's life.

Yet one look at the photo reenacting their night together had him hard as steel for Sable. And for his part, he didn't see why they shouldn't indulge in something that made them both feel good. But he guessed she hadn't reached that same conclusion based on the careful way she'd conducted herself with him since his return from LA.

Well, until now.

Because he wasn't alone in enjoying this kiss.

He stroked over the seam of her lips, demanding access. And she not only surrendered, she made hot demands of her own, her hands lifting to wrap around his neck, to pull him closer and take the kiss deeper.

And while he was game for both those things, but not at the cost of her retreating from him even more tomorrow.

Breaking the kiss with what felt like superhuman effort, he let his forehead fall to hers while they caught their breath.

"Sable." His gaze dropped to her lush lips still damp from his tongue and he had to close his eyes to keep from returning to that sweet spot for another taste.

"Mmm?" The sound she made in answer only tempted him more.

Her fingers were still locked behind his neck and, as he opened his eyes again, his attention shifted to the way her raised arms lifted her breasts toward him. The buttons holding together her white dress practically called to his hand to unfasten them. To free her body so he could worship her curves properly.

"Two months ago when we were together, I told you I'd stay away so things could cool off between us." How many times had he regretted that offer? But at the time, he wasn't sure how else to counterbalance the fact that she was technically his employee. He hadn't wanted their night together to be tainted by that.

"I remember," she said on a breathy exhale, her knees shifting around his legs, reminding him of how thoroughly he'd invaded her personal space. "You were as good as your word."

He couldn't quite read her tone, and damn it, they needed to be sure they understood each other now.

"We're relocating this conversation to the couch where I can look you in the eye." Shuffling back a step, he tucked one arm under her knees and slid the other under her arms, lifting her off the barstool to carry her into the living room.

"Oh." She let out a startled gasp, steadying herself with a hand on his shoulder. "Really? I'm pregnant, Roman, not bedridden. I can handle walking."

"It might not be wise to discuss beds right now. Not when I want you in mine this badly." He couldn't help looking down at where his hand wrapped around her thigh, and imagining how fast he could undress her so that he could touch even more of her.

She felt good against him. Like she belonged there.

But he shut down that thought fast. It was one thing to want her in his bed. It was something else altogether to consider a deeper connection. Because he wouldn't dishonor the vow he'd made to his wife that way.

Maybe that was why he settled her in the corner of the rolled-arm sofa and sat down beside her, instead of draping her over his lap the way he wanted. Still, he couldn't totally take his hands off her, either. He turned toward her, resting his right hand on her knee just below the hem of her dress.

"Okay." He let his fingers dip between her knees. But when she sucked in a rapid breath, he pulled back. "Clearly we need to revisit the parameters of our original deal. Things didn't cool off after two months. If anything, I want you more than ever."

"Same," she murmured. Her hazel eyes shot to his after a moment, as if gauging his reaction. "That is, I agree about the heat level. Still…hot."

The sticky drawl of her words pulled at him as she wrapped a dark curl around her finger. With another woman, Roman might have thought the move was a deliberate flirtation. But Sable looked down, and the way she worked her lower lip with her teeth made her seem nervous. Uneasy.

And that, he couldn't abide.

"Hey." He cupped her jaw and turned her face toward him. "We don't have to act on it just because it's there. I'm going to be right there with you through this pregnancy whether you want to share my bed again or not. You know that, don't you?"

"I do." She nodded as if she'd understood that all along, but it unsettled him that some of her tension seemed to slide off her shoulders with his reassurance. "It's just the chemistry is so strong, I almost can't think when you're near me. What if a return to intimacy makes it all the more difficult to be objective about what happens next? And the stakes are higher than ever now, so I don't want to make a bad judgment call."

"I'm man enough to admit that while I don't *like* that answer, I respect the hell out of you for it." He appreciated her honesty, too. Because the attraction had the power to flatten both of them, which would be easy to prove with one kiss.

"You do?" Letting go of the lock of hair, she glanced up at him, her intelligent eyes tracking his.

"Hell yes. You're being protective of our future relationship as parents. I want you to trust your instincts." Even though his body was already threatening a mutiny at the prospect of not being with her tonight. "The only answer is that we wait."

Hell, even saying the words out loud hurt.

"We wait," she repeated on a breathy sigh, sounding about as enthusiastic about the plan as he felt, which made him smile.

And gave him an idea. Because he didn't want to

leave her unsatisfied. Not when she craved something from him that he could provide.

"Just because we hold off on sex doesn't mean I need to leave you unfulfilled." He allowed his fingers to unfurl again, tracing a circle just inside her knee.

Her breath caught. He was close enough to hear that tiny, staggered inhalation, and he liked what it told him.

"W-what do you mean?" She tipped her head back a fraction, her dark hair sliding sideways with the movement. The soft swish of silky locks against the leather made him want to wrap the dark length of hair around his hand. To tug her head back for another kiss.

"I think you know." He glided his fingers higher, beneath the dress's hem. "But I'm glad to be more explicit. Especially if hearing the things I want to do to you will add to your pleasure."

Her pulse throbbed harder, a reaction he could feel against his thumb on the inside of her thigh.

"Touching each other is an intimacy all its own," she said carefully, even while her pupils dilated.

"It's a middle ground," he countered, stilling his hand until he was certain of what she wanted to happen next. "I can take the edge off for you, and we keep our clothes on."

He could tell she liked the idea by the way her gaze fell to his mouth, her breath coming faster.

"What about you?" Her fingers grazed the buttons on his shirt, and his brain promptly supplied other uses for her touch.

"This isn't about me." He was resolute on that point, more than happy to delay his gratification in favor of hers. "I'm not the one going through pregnancy. It's only fair I do something for you while you carry the greater physical burden."

The corners of her full lips kicked up. "You make a compelling case."

He allowed his fingers to press lightly into her skin where he still touched her. The room was utterly still except for the dull ticking of a clock on the fireplace mantel. "And I didn't even use my most persuasive arguments."

She pressed her legs together, squeezing his hand lightly between her thighs. Her white dress took on a blue cast from the city lights filtering through the window behind her.

"Then by all means." She breathed the words over his mouth, arching her back to get closer. "Keep convincing me."

Hell. Yes.

Hunger for her surged through him when she gave him the green light. He needed to see her eyes blaze with passion, to hear her lips chant his name. She might prevent him from providing for her in other ways, but in this, he would never fail.

* * *

Sable shivered at the look in Roman's dark eyes.

It was knowing and primally male. A seasoned warrior sizing up the castle he was about to lay siege to. Was it wrong that she wanted to revel in being the object of that lust, just for a few stolen moments? All while keeping her clothes on?

She was maintaining some boundaries, after all. There would be no deeper intimacy tonight. Just Roman taking her body to levels of pleasure she'd only ever experienced with him.

And, oh God, it already felt so good to have his palm splayed over her thigh, his fingers drifting closer to where she desperately needed him. His wide shoulders loomed over hers as he leaned closer to kiss her.

"I hardly know where to taste you first," he said against her lips, the words vibrating up her spine since they sat so close. "Here." He sucked her lower lip into his mouth before letting it slide free again. "Or here." He licked his way down her throat, the warm suction of his mouth pulling a moan from her. "I just know you taste so good everywhere."

His fingers grazed the edge of her panties beneath her dress, one knuckle stroking up her center over the silk barrier as he spoke.

"Roman." She shuddered at the feel of him there, desire turning into a sharp, empty ache. "Please."

"I need you closer to me first." He scooped her up and moved her to his lap, spreading his legs wide to cradle her while her head rested against his shoulder. "I want to feel you against me when you find your pleasure."

She wasn't about to argue since it felt amazing to be surrounded by so much male heat and strength. But the need to wriggle out of her clothes so he could touch more of her was growing fiercer by the second. And if she felt restrained, she could only imagine what a torment this must be for him. The proof of his need was a hot brand against her hip. It would be so easy to turn in his arms and straddle his hips to give them both what they craved.

"Is this better?" She arched up to kiss along his jaw. Lick the skin beneath his ear.

"Much. Now I have a front seat to see you come apart for me." He cupped her sex, stroking her with the heel of his hand and propelling her higher. "It's been too long since the last time. I've had months to think about all the ways I wanted to touch you if I ever got the chance again."

She wanted to focus on his words, but it was impossible with his fingers working her into a frenzy of sensation, gently pinching and kneading, stroking, and plucking. Her breath came too fast to catch and she tightened her grip on his shoulders.

"I missed you, too," she admitted, her defenses

low while her need for him built. Besides, they were talking about sex. Right? "I missed this."

"I'm going to prove how well I can take care of you, Sable," he whispered against her ear before nipping the flesh there. "You never need to go unsatisfied."

He slowed his touches beneath her dress and edged aside her underwear to plunge two fingers inside her. Her body stilled for an extended, breathless moment, her spine going taut. Then sensation rocked her, ripples of pleasure pulsing one after the other. Her feminine muscles shook and trembled with the force of her orgasm.

She might have screamed. She definitely called his name. More than once. The waves of release just kept coming, until she was wrung out and tucking her face into his shoulder to try to collect herself.

Slowly she became aware of Roman kissing the top of her head. Easing her underwear back into place.

All while his body remained rock-hard and in need of release.

"It seems unfair—" she began, but he bent to kiss her before she could complete the thought.

"Just…let me hold you a little longer." His tone sounded off, somehow, but she guessed that it was because he was still battling his own desire.

He didn't meet her gaze, though, so she found it

difficult to gauge his mood, let alone pull herself back together.

Being together this way would only lead her to more feelings for the father of her child, and she wasn't ready for that.

And no matter what Roman said about wanting to provide for her throughout her pregnancy, she suspected that the events of the evening—the whole day, for that matter—rocked him, too.

"I should go." She shifted again, and this time he didn't stop her when she slid off his lap.

When she met his dark gaze, his expression was shuttered. So even looking right into his eyes, she couldn't get any read on him or what he might be thinking.

He had secrets, she realized. Or, at the very least, something he wasn't telling her. The idea pricked at her sharply, but she trusted the instinct.

"When will I see you again?" he asked, coming to his feet.

He didn't touch her this time, which had her emotional radar pinging all over the place.

She focused on his question, knowing she'd have to find a way to balance her feelings for Roman with practical concerns. The sooner she figured out how to do that, the better.

"Normally there are only two ultrasound appointments per pregnancy, but the obstetrician agreed to another one in two weeks." She retrieved her purse and slung the bag over one shoulder.

"I can't go another two weeks without seeing you." His brows drew together in concern. Or maybe confusion. "And I'll drive you home, Sable."

"That's not necessary." The sooner she resurrected boundaries, the better.

"I insist." He found his phone and keyed something in before pocketing it again. "A driver will meet us downstairs."

"Fine. I just need my coat." She moved toward the door, feeling suddenly adrift and out of place in his wealthy world.

Not just because she was an intern in his company who was now expecting his child. But also because she might need to leave New York in a few months' time, while he was contemplating a second home here even as he enjoyed a space like this one with the kind of view that cost millions. How was she going to share a child with someone like Roman, who could afford to order his world however he chose?

"Sable." He wrapped an arm around her waist and hauled her backward against him. "Don't shut me out. We'll come up with a good plan for the future, but we have to do it together. Right?"

He spoke the words against the top of her head, and some of the tension drained from her shoulders at the feel of his chest pressed to her. Which made no sense since being physical with him also accounted for the awkward turn things had taken between them. Hadn't it?

"Once I pass the twelve-week mark, I'll be better able to focus on the future." She was already attached to this baby. Making premature plans with Roman could only hurt more later if anything happened to endanger the pregnancy now. Her heart had only just begun to heal. She needed more time to shore up her boundaries.

"I understand." He turned her in his arms, his strong hands gripping her shoulders for a moment before falling away. "So let's use the next two weeks to get to know each other better. Feel more comfortable with one another to pave the way for a good parenting relationship down the road."

She wanted to ask him why he'd checked out on her tonight after he touched her. Where had his thoughts flown in those moments when he wouldn't meet her gaze? But she wasn't ready to make herself vulnerable that way yet, to reveal the insecurity his inattention had stirred.

Besides, he'd been thoughtful and generous to her in many ways this evening. She wouldn't discount those efforts. She just needed to keep a careful rein on her feelings so she didn't end up reading more into the situation than what was really there.

"Okay. Two weeks to find our way," she agreed.

She folded her arms across the front of body, suddenly feeling a need for more distance to regain her objectivity. "How do you suggest we implement this plan of yours?"

He stepped away to retrieve her lightweight trench coat, then settled it on her shoulders, all with minimal contact. Was he reading her signals? Or was he throwing off his own now that they'd reached the negotiation phase of the evening?

Exhaustion from the long, demanding day hit her all at once, bound up with the mental weariness from trying to decipher Roman.

"How much of New York have you seen since you've been here? We could play tourist for a day. Take in some sights." He grabbed a set of keys before escorting her to the door, then doubled back to the kitchen. "I almost forgot about the cake," he explained as he took out a small paper bag from one of the catering sacks that remained on the counter. "Never let it be said I sent you home without dessert."

"I wouldn't dream of it." Her cheeks warmed at the memory of how they'd spent the time after dinner instead. When he returned to her, paper bag in hand, she shoved aside the thought to focus on his earlier question. "And I'd love to play tourist for a day. I've been too busy working to see the sights."

Plus, if they were out sightseeing, they couldn't get sidetracked by the chemistry that was always simmering in the background, ready to boil over at the least provocation.

"In that case, can you keep your Saturday open?" he asked as he opened and held the door for her, readying himself to accompany her home.

"I can." That would leave her with three days to shore up her defenses before she saw him again. Three days of mental pep talks to ensure she kept their relationship more on a friendly level. Less passion-fueled.

"Perfect. I'll pick you up at noon and we'll make a day of it." His hand grazed her back as they stepped into the elevator cabin together, and just that small touch sent new shivers along her skin.

Who did she think she was kidding?

Three days wouldn't be nearly enough.

Seven

Friday evening, before her date with Roman the next day, Sable was already dreaming up excuses for canceling. She peeled off her earbuds as she trekked out of the Fulton Street subway station and headed toward Fort Greene Park, anxiety dogging her. She tried to think of something that Roman wouldn't see right through.

The truth was she didn't trust herself around all that potent sexuality, especially when it came wrapped up in so much concern for her. Well, for her *baby*. Maybe it was all the pregnancy hormones that made her swoon at the memory of Roman's obvious care for her health and the well-being of their child. But the fact that he wanted to be at her doctor appointments, that it mattered to him if she was eating healthy and sleeping well, and that he'd felt compelled to celebrate the ultrasound had all slid right past her defenses.

Add to that the way his touch could launch her body into the stratosphere? The man was her kryptonite. And she didn't have any more idea how to set boundaries now than she had two days ago when she'd come apart in his arms.

Her brownstone came into view as the lights of evening started to illuminate the darkening street. Sable's nerves twisted at the thought of letting him get any closer. Physically, sure, but even more so emotionally. She couldn't afford to lose her hard-won sense of self after the nightmare of her divorce following the miscarriage.

She was almost at her stoop when the blare of rock music hit her ears. A guitar solo wailed through an open window on the garden floor. There was a bedroom down there, but it had been vacated three weeks ago by a dancer who'd nailed down a spot as a Rockette and was now sharing an apartment with a few other performers in the theater district.

Had someone else moved in? Blair Wescott, the makeup artist and Mini-Me version of Cybil Deschamps, had already claimed the big bedroom on the third floor right below Sable.

She hurried up the steps to the entrance and let herself inside, more than ready to throw herself into any new roommate intrigue to take her mind off Roman and her situation. Whenever she wasn't thinking about how to build a secure future for her child, how to reconcile her professional dreams with her new reality, or when to tell Marcel she was expecting, she obsessed about Roman and what kind of relationship she should be building with him. She hadn't realized until she heard the music that she craved girl talk. Stat.

"Hello?" she called once she was inside the foyer. Her voice echoed hollowly in the entrance hallway as she peered into the great room. There wasn't a lot of furniture in the space.

Cybil had left them the basics—a couple of vintage couches and chairs to fill the huge great room with high ceilings—but there wasn't much in the way of rugs, paintings or decor. The original parquet floors shone dully in the light coming in from the street since no one had switched on any lamps up here. Laughter floated up the staircase from the garden level, audible in the momentary reprieve between rock songs.

"Hello?" she called again as she started downstairs, enticed by the scent of popcorn.

"It's my long-lost fourth floor roommate." Tana Blackstone appeared at the base of the staircase.

Petite and delicate, Tana had a fairy-like beauty with her glossy brown hair and heart-shaped face. But unless she was auditioning for a part, she took tough-girl fashion seriously. When she wasn't in leather and spikes, she draped herself in oversize flannel shirts, army-navy store finds, and combat boots. Her nods to femininity were dyed hair tips in an ever-changing rainbow of colors and glittery eye makeup.

Sable had to admire her commitment to an aesthetic. Today, Tana wore a T-shirt with a cartoon superhero, spiked leather bracelets, and jeans with more holes than fabric, which showed off spiderweb-patterned tights beneath. Her hair had green tips to match her eyeshadow and a tiny stud in her nose.

From behind Tana, their new roommate peeked her head around a wainscoted column that separated the kitchen from the hallway at the base of the stairs.

"We needed a Friday happy hour," Blair explained as she raised a martini glass containing a frosty-looking yellow drink layered on top of a red base. "Ready for a raspberry lemon drop?"

Tana waved Sable toward the all-white kitchen. "You have to try one. Blair is a grand wizard mixologist. These things look like works of art and they taste even better."

"Oh. Um." Sable would have given her right arm for one of those gorgeous drinks two months ago.

She hesitated as she searched for a believable excuse. "I can't. I'm on a mega-strict cleanse."

"On a Friday?" Blair used one hand to hoist herself onto the marble counter next to the blender where she'd obviously been working. There were a few liquor bottles, and lemons and raspberries spilled over the edge of a cutting board.

Blair Westcott looked far more at ease today in a pair of purple leggings and a slouchy pink yoga top, her platinum blond hair in one long braid that swung over her shoulder. With her high-top sneakers and her face scrubbed clean, she looked more like a college co-ed than the sought-after makeup artist that Cybil Deschamps had personally chosen to work for her cosmetics company.

Spotting the bowl of popcorn on the counter near Blair, Sable scooped up a handful to nosh on.

Tana tapped the screen of her phone, lowering the volume on the head-banging music coming from the Bluetooth speaker balanced on the coffee maker. "We're drinking to my second callback for a soap opera role, which could be the difference between me getting to afford one more month in New York or—not."

Sable empathized more than Tana could know, considering how her own days in this expensive city were numbered now that she was expecting a baby. Unless she accepted Roman's offer.

Which she couldn't.

"You're going to get the part," Blair told Tana firmly. Then, she pointed her martini glass toward Sable and explained, "I ran lines with her before today's callback, and she's great."

Tana scoffed, but something in her expression showed her pleasure at the compliment.

Sable felt guilty that she'd offered her roommates so little of her time. Blair had only been living here for a few days and had already jumped in to help, while Sable barely knew what Tana did each day. Or maybe it wasn't guilt so much as simple regret that she hadn't taken the time to enjoy the camaraderie of things like Friday happy hours with these women who had the potential to be good friends. She'd been so invested in her job, spending all her extra time on creating content for Zayn social media, that she'd ignored her personal interests at a time when she might have really benefited from girlfriends.

Especially now, when this world was slipping away from her too quickly.

"I could at least have something nonalcoholic with you," she announced, stashing her bag on an open shelf of cookbooks below the breakfast bar that overlooked the dining room. "Second callbacks deserve celebrating."

"I made fresh lemonade," Blair said. "It's in the fridge."

"Wait until you see this," Tana added, darting past Sable to reach the refrigerator first so she could open the door for her. "Look."

The high-end appliance had been cleaned out and organized; the white interior was gleaming and the thinned-out offerings were now easy to see. In the middle of the tallest shelf sat a hand-painted glass pitcher filled with ice cubes and fresh lemon slices.

"As in you *made* lemonade? From scratch?" Sable lifted out the pitcher, exchanging looks with Tana, whose expression communicated equal enthusiasm for their new housemate.

"You know it's just three ingredients, right?" Blair opened a cupboard and located a hand-painted glass that matched the pitcher. "It's been fun exploring the kitchen. Cybil has everything in here."

Sable continued to stare into the refrigerator, suddenly ravenous at the sight of food and wishing she'd come up with a different excuse for not drinking. She hid a sigh as she poured her lemonade, returned the pitcher to the shelf, and closed the door.

Lifting her glass, she faced Blair and Tana. "To second callbacks."

"And staying in New York," Tana added as she raised hers, the silver skull on her leather wrist cuff glinting in the light from the Art Deco–style pendant lamp.

"And new friends." Blair slid off the counter to

clink her glass with theirs. "I don't know about you all, but I'm far from home, and I appreciate the girl time. Cheers, *chicas*."

"Cheers." Sable's throat tightened; she agreed with the sentiment even if she wouldn't be able to enjoy it for long.

Didn't she owe it to herself and her child to have more of a network? Especially since she would be doing her portion of the childrearing alone. Sure, Roman wanted to share the duties with her, but that just meant handing off their baby to him so he could take his turn at parenting—alone. And when she got the child back, she'd have to navigate the decisions and responsibilities by herself, as well.

As the reality of that set in—along with hunger pangs for more than just popcorn—Sable decided she didn't want to keep her pregnancy a secret any longer. Was that unfair since she'd asked Roman to keep it quiet until the twelve-week appointment?

Yes. But he wasn't carrying the baby. He didn't have the same burdens she did, let alone the same anxieties. Even though he might share some of her fears about a miscarriage, he couldn't possibly know the devastation of losing a longed-for pregnancy.

It was on the tip of her tongue to confess the truth when the doorbell chimed.

"Did you order a pizza?" Sable asked, blurting out the only possibility that came to mind.

Tana was already jogging up the steps to answer the door. Blair was shaking her head when they heard voices at the front door—Tana's and a man's. It wasn't Roman. Sable would have known that particular tone anywhere. But she could see in Blair's face that the woman recognized who it was. Her cheeks went pink even as the rest of her skin paled. She swallowed reflexively.

A curious response.

"Blair?" Tana called down the steps. "Lucas Deschamps is here and he's asking for you."

Sable bit back a smile as Blair swore and then paced twice across the kitchen before heading upstairs.

Apparently Friday night happy hour was over. And maybe it was just as well, since now Sable could finally make herself some dinner. Soon, she'd tell her new friends about the baby.

But first, she had to get through her date with Roman tomorrow without things becoming heated. She hoped it would be easier now that she understood Roman was keeping a piece of himself locked away from her. More than once, she'd relived those moments when his expression had gone shuttered after they'd gotten intimate two nights ago. She'd had the sense he was hiding something from her, and the anxiety about what that might be had only grown in their time apart.

Maybe the memory of that feeling—the way he'd kept her at arm's length right after he'd taken her to sensual heights—would help her resist him tomorrow.

Besides, they were sightseeing. As long as they remained in public, there would be no chance of clothes coming off or boundaries coming down.

And her wounded feelings from two days ago would give her the extra defenses she needed around him.

"I wish I could take photos of your brother's designs with this as a backdrop," Sable commented as she strolled through the Cloisters museum, pausing briefly to admire the view of the Hudson River outside one of the doors. "Everything would look more elegant in this setting."

She made an expansive gesture with one arm, indicating the L-shaped arcade overlooking well-tended gardens planted with hundreds of species used for food, medicine or—according to the literature—magic in the Middle Ages.

Roman followed her, more captivated by the woman than the art and architecture. Spring bloomed outside the open arcade, with vibrant flowers and droning bees drunk on too much pollen. But the lush silhouette of Sable in a full yellow skirt and fitted white T-shirt drew his eye the most. The day had been relaxed and fun, with Sable taking as much pleasure from the architectural elements salvaged from medieval abbeys and churches as she did from the unicorn tapestries and the profusion of plant life. They'd played "I spy" with the huge tapestries, finding cats and frogs, hidden initials and dragonflies. She'd revealed a deep love of art that her husband apparently hadn't shared, making Roman all the more glad he'd brought her here for a day of sightseeing.

A day to get to know her better and—he hoped—start planning a workable future for raising a child together. So far, he'd been able to shove aside the ever-present attraction enough to put her at ease, and he was damned grateful she hadn't brought up the way their last date had morphed from dinner to him touching her. As much as he'd lobbied to give her that kind of release, and as much as he absolutely had wanted it, he hadn't bargained on the feelings that swamped him afterward. The need to pull her into his arms. To take her to bed for more than just sex. To hold her. Comfort her.

To lay his hand on the place where his child grew.

Those needs had rattled the hell out of him, reminding him there was risk involved every time he succumbed to the chemistry with Sable.

Now she glanced at him over her shoulder, making him realize he'd been lost in thought about what happened next.

"I'm glad you approve of this place," he finally answered, his hand moving automatically to the small of her back as they headed deeper into the unique building made up of reconstructed cloisters from medieval Europe. "The park is beautiful, too. I thought we'd take a walk on the paths whenever you're ready." He'd brought a picnic to share with her and left the hamper in the car while they toured the museum.

"Sounds good," she agreed, pausing inside the cool, shadowy interior where stone steps led down into a room they hadn't yet explored. "This must be the Gothic chapel. The colors of the stained glass are so pretty."

Roman followed, his gaze snagging on the tomb effigies laid out around the chapel, while Sable checked her phone for notes on the self-guided tour she'd downloaded for the day. He hadn't realized he'd halted his steps until she turned to look back at him.

"Are you coming?" She observed him, her head tilted to one side, dark hair sliding over her shoulder.

He couldn't imagine what she might see reflected on his face as the somber ambience of the chapel took hold of him, memories of another chapel weighing his feet like lead. He was standing beside a tomb featuring a sculpture of a woman in silent repose, her hands clasped just above her waist and her head resting forever on a pillow of cold limestone. And just like that he was catapulted back in time, to a casket he'd never wanted to stand beside.

Was it the atmosphere created by the stained glass and statues of saints around the chapel that brought back so vividly the day he'd laid his wife to rest? Or was it the effigy of the noblewoman in her gown and jewelry, a coin purse at her waist, that reminded him of Annette's family squabbling about which of her dresses to send to the funeral home? They'd fought about the outfit as if it mattered, as if it made any difference to the woman he'd loved, who was gone forever.

A bead of cold sweat rolled down his temple.

"Roman?" Sable's voice sounded far away now, and distorted as if she were speaking underwater.

He took in a breath to answer, but the feeling of claustrophobia increased, as if the walls were pressing in and there was no air to spare. His fingers moved to his throat, as if to loosen a collar or tie, or whatever was making his airway feel constricted. But there was nothing there.

Just skin gone clammy above the open neck of his button-down.

"Excuse me." He thought he said the words aloud, but couldn't be sure. He only knew he needed to get outside.

Away from the tombs and the dark, quiet chapel. *Now.*

Bolting up the stairs, he crossed an arcade, passed the tapestries room and followed exit signs to the east side of the building. He went down a long ramp toward a set of double doors and barreled through one of them, craving sunshine and fresh air. A breath that wasn't haunted by the past.

On the pavement out front, he dragged in one lungful after another, waiting for his head to clear. For the cold clamminess on his skin to disappear. He shoved a weary hand into his hair and scraped his fingertips over his scalp, willing some warmth to return to his body.

A moment later, he heard light footsteps approaching behind him. He didn't know how he knew it was Sable when a hundred other people were there around him, entering and exiting the museum or exploring the park. Yet he knew without turning that she was the one drawing near. The back of his neck prickled with awareness.

And at this moment more than ever, it felt like disloyalty to his wife's memory. He briefly squeezed his eyes shut in an effort to get his head together before he turned and faced her.

The tender concern in her hazel eyes slid right past his defenses, reminding him that Sable was a good person. None of his screwed-up feelings were her fault, and he owed her an explanation.

"Should we head home?" Sunlight streamed

through her dark hair, burnishing the glossy locks to show subtle caramel strands. "I can drive if you don't feel well."

"I'm better," he assured her, taking her cool fingers in his. "Are you still up for that walk?"

He hoped it would help level him out. Calm his still racing heart. Plus, he really wanted to banish the shadows in Sable's eyes. Shadows he'd put there, when he'd been trying so hard to make the day all about her. But he knew he owed her an explanation, and he couldn't very well provide it here in front of the swarm of visitors.

"Are you sure?" She took a step closer to him, the yellow outer layer of her floaty skirt brushing against his calf as she moved. "I don't mind calling it a day."

"No. I'm fine." Squeezing her fingers gently in his, he lifted her hand to his lips and kissed the backs of her knuckles, trying like hell to turn his thoughts around. "Let's find a spot with a good river view."

After a moment she nodded, walking with him along the winding paths and stone steps of Fort Tryon Park, the highest point in Manhattan. They remained quiet while they passed through flower beds and crossed an access road, until they reached a low stone wall that separated the lane from the cliffs beyond.

His car was parked close by, but he wasn't ready to retrieve the food yet. He needed to talk to Sable first. Scouting a good spot to sit and have some privacy, he followed the low wall until he found a flat rock on the other side. The promontory offered a good view of the Hudson River.

"Here. Do you mind if we have a seat for a few minutes?" He pointed out the place he had in mind.

"Sure. I might need a hand over the barrier." Her gaze flicked to him carefully, as if she was waiting for him to sprint away from her again.

Roman climbed the low stone wall first and then reached back for her, keeping her steady while she navigated the divider. She hopped down beside him, then took a seat on the smooth, flat rock. She folded her skirt around her and drew her knees up a little. She fixed her gaze on the water as a barge moved north, slowly passing the Palisades on the other side of the river. He joined her, sitting close to her but not touching.

"This is gorgeous. You'd never know we were in the city here." She withdrew her phone and snapped a couple of photos of the river and, south of them, the George Washington Bridge.

He wished he could lose himself in a conversation about the scenery. And, hell, he appreciated the way she gave him an out from talking about what had set him off back there. She had to know something was wrong and yet she was letting him have some space. But she deserved to know the truth.

"You must be wondering what happened in the chapel." His jaw felt tight. As if his body physically resisted telling the story. He scrubbed a hand over his face.

"I am. But if you'd rather not discuss it—"

"I need to." Of course, that wasn't entirely true. He started again. "That is. You should know."

He stared out at the water as he heard her set aside her phone. He felt rather than saw her tip her head toward him. Waiting. Listening.

"The tombs reminded me of someone I lost. It's been five years, so I hadn't really expected that strong a reaction." In some ways, Annette's death seemed so recent. But he'd been living without her for five years and three months.

He'd had the grief counseling. He'd thought he'd made his peace. But the baby news had stirred it up for him.

"I'm sorry," Sable offered quietly, slipping her hand over his to lay her palm on the back of his fingers.

"Thank you. It's been on my mind more recently because of the pregnancy. I think that's why the memories came back so strongly today." Even in the worst of his grief, he'd never had that claustrophobic feeling that had come over him today. That sense he couldn't breathe.

She went very still beside him. "Whom did you lose?"

He couldn't tell what she was thinking, but something in her tone made him glance over at her. She was pale. Worried.

Did she suspect what he was going to say? Even if she guessed he'd been married before, he wasn't sure why that would upset her. Not when they were only just getting to know each other, and she'd been so definite about not leaping into a more romantic relationship with him.

Knowing there was no way around it, he admitted what he hadn't shared with any other woman who'd passed through his life in the years since Annette's death.

"My wife." His gaze held Sable's. "I was married for fifteen months before she died during a failed heart transplant surgery."

Eight

Roman was a widower.

Sable allowed the revelation to sink in while the spring sun warmed her bare calves. Birds chirped in the trees overhead. Sunbeams glittered on the Hudson River below them. But the happy bloom of oblivious nature no longer gave the day the same glow that she'd felt earlier. Now she understood why Roman's skin had felt cold to the touch while they were inside the dim Gothic chapel.

He grieved for a woman he'd loved. A woman he clearly loved still.

"I'm—" *Stunned you never mentioned a previ-*

ous marriage. But this wasn't about her. She could see for herself how much he mourned his wife. "I'm so sorry, Roman."

She didn't trust herself to say much more until she'd wrapped her head around this new disclosure. Her hand remained on top of his, and she stared down at it now, feeling self-conscious about the gesture. Feeling like an intruder in his grief when she wasn't the woman who held his heart. Giving his hand a last squeeze, she let go and tucked her palms between her knees.

"I should have told you about Annette before. I almost did when we talked about your ex. But we ended up talking about the miscarriage and my thoughts shifted to the baby. And worry about you." The raw honesty of the words pulled at her, forcing her out of her own thoughts to focus on him.

"Tell me about her." She needed to know more. After that night she'd had dinner with him, she'd sensed he'd been holding back from her—keeping secrets. Now she understood this was it.

If he'd been holding his marriage close and not sharing with her, she suspected there was a reason for that. And it wasn't that he just hadn't found a way to introduce the topic.

Beside her, Roman draped his wrists over his knees, shoulders dropping.

"We met when she was still in college. I'd already

graduated, but I went back to campus to speak at the invitation of one of my finance professors. Annette was one of his star students, on track for a big career after interning at a prestigious equity firm. She asked to speak with me about the industry and we—" He broke off, shaking his head as if he didn't want to reveal intimate details.

Sable's throat burned. She wouldn't allow herself to feel jealousy for a dead woman. But the sight of Roman's obvious all-encompassing love for someone else hurt far more than it should have. What room would he have left in his emotions for anyone else?

"You said she needed a heart transplant?" she ventured, trying to give him a way out of whatever he was remembering right now.

Nodding, he took a long breath. "She was born with a heart problem that required a transplant when she was just two years old. Transplanted organs have a shelf life, and although she'd done well with hers, she understood that there would come a time she'd need another one." His head dipped as he paused, lines carving into his forehead while he seemed to gather his thoughts. "She took antirejection medicine her whole life. Took great care of herself, and had such an amazing outlook."

The unevenness of his voice touched Sable, chastising her for the earlier flash of jealousy she'd experienced. She tipped her head to his shoulder, needing to give him some kind of comfort while she waited for him to continue.

"After the wedding, she had problems almost immediately. But I was traveling quite a bit those first few months, and she had a new job, so I didn't know about the signs." He sounded harsh. Almost angry. Did he blame himself somehow for her health issues? "When I found out about them, I insisted she see her doctor, and we cut short a delayed honeymoon trip to the Seychelles that we took six months after we married. We flew home and her cardiologist put her on a transplant list right away."

Her head still on his shoulder, Sable threaded her arm through his, her gaze tracking a speedboat slicing through the river spread out below them. She breathed in Roman's scent, which brought to mind woodsmoke and pine.

"Did it take all that time to obtain a heart?" She didn't know anything about organ transplants, but if they were together for fifteen months, that would mean it took nine months to find a donor.

"No. She was scheduled for a transplant six months later, but there was a problem with the donated organ and her doctor couldn't use it. So she went on the list again." His voice dropped. "When the next one arrived three months later, it seemed like a good fit. But—" He broke off before finishing in a rush. "Her body rejected it."

"How unfair for her. For you, too. And her family. What a traumatic way to lose a loved one."

"There are no good ways," he muttered dryly, his muscles still strung tight with tension where Sable touched him.

She lifted her head to see his face, and blinked at the stark pain in his brown eyes. Her fingers pressed into his forearm, and she wished she could take away some of the hurt with her touch. But she knew instinctively she wasn't going to make a dent in those feelings.

"Still, you had every reason to think you'd bring her home after surgery. She was young and vital. If she kept the first heart for over twenty years, you surely thought you'd have more time with her once she received the second."

He wrenched his gaze away from hers, shaking his head slowly, as if it weighed heavily on his shoulders.

"The risks are high every time. We both knew that. But— I would have given anything for even one more year. One more month." The trace of bitterness in his tone, of love, was unmistakable.

And it sharpened her understanding of her place in Roman's life. She might be the mother of his child, but it was clear that another woman still held his love. The realization sank home, like a cold weight deep in the pit of her belly.

Not that it should matter, since she'd been insistent on keeping him at arm's length to protect herself.

Turned out she needn't have worried when Roman had no intention of a deeper relationship than shared parenting with her anyhow.

"And you think the news of this pregnancy brought the grief close to the surface?" She knew it was foolish of her to ask when her emotions were already unsteady.

Major understatement.

She *ached* with knowing how deep his love and loyalty ran to his late wife, and how far she'd always been from experiencing a love like that. She certainly hadn't had that with Jack. And she'd never have a chance to experience it with Roman.

"Annette wanted children," he said simply, in a way that made it clear he would have moved heaven and earth to fulfill her wishes. "We agreed we would contact an adoption agency on our first anniversary. Then we delayed it, thinking there would be time after her surgery."

Sable withdrew her arm from his, unsure she could offer comfort right now when she was feeling a hole open up inside her. "I can see why this pregnancy would bring a lot of mixed feelings for you, Roman."

"It doesn't," he said fiercely, his hands clamping on her shoulders as he shifted positions, seating himself in front of her so he could look her in the eye. "There are no mixed feelings about this baby. I will love this child and so will you." He waited a moment, as if allowing her to absorb the weight of that. Then, more gently, he stroked her hair from her face, combing it behind her ear. "I already do."

Her eyes stung. The silence stretched between them until she didn't trust herself to speak for the emotions bubbling up inside her. So she nodded a little frantically in agreement. "Okay," she managed in a raspy whisper as she tried not to cry. "Yes."

Roman took her in with an intense look in his dark eyes, making her wonder what he saw in her expression. She hoped he could only glean her love of their child and not the misplaced envy for his love, which she couldn't have for herself. It was foolish. She was foolish.

"Hormones," she finally said, as a couple of tears slipped free even as she attempted to laugh. "It must be the pregnancy hormones."

Whatever he saw in her face, it seemed to push him to make a decision. He gave a thoughtful nod before he spoke.

"Come on." He stood, took her hands and hauled her to her feet. "I've heard there's a surefire cure for that. But first I need to know, what's your favorite flavor of ice cream?"

In the week since he'd last spent time with Sable at the Cloisters, Roman's mood had plummeted, getting worse and worse on a daily basis.

Every frustrating hour of that time weighed heavily on his shoulders, a weight he dragged around whether he was seeing properties with his Realtor, taking conference calls with his office in Los Angeles, or reviewing the books for the fashion house in Marcel's cramped back office at Zayn Designs.

Like now.

Parked behind his temporary desk, scrolling through his brother's business expenses on the computer, he could hear the easy rapport between Marcel and his assistants—Sable included—filtering through the open door. It made no sense that Roman felt a surge of jealousy every time Marcel teased a laugh out of Sable, the musical sound stirring equal parts gratitude for her happiness and possessiveness that he hadn't been the man to cause it. The caveman instincts were utterly new to him and unique to his relationship with Sable. He told himself it was because she was carrying his child.

There could be no other reason to account for the tangled-up reactions he hadn't even experienced with Annette, a woman he loved more than life.

Scowling, he ignored the latest round of laughter floating over the strains of a Duke Ellington song. The theme of the day seemed to be jazz and big band music. Roman had no idea what they were working on in the design studio now that it was past five o'clock on a Friday, but it sounded a whole lot more fun than reviewing endless columns of poorly organized numbers, many of which struck him as unnecessary expenditures.

"Sotheby's Auction House?" Roman called through the door, needing clarification on a staggeringly costly purchase.

"Original artwork for the flagship store," Marcel shouted back, before his voice returned to a normal pitch as he gave instructions to someone about adding more beadwork to a gown.

Roman's head pounded at the response, since Marcel didn't even have a property purchased for his store, let alone a finalized business plan for a dedicated retail space. Roman wanted Zayn Designs to be a global success—needed for it to be since he'd invested much of his personal savings into financing the venture—but his brother refused half of Roman's business advice. It made him question why he bothered remaining in New York when Marcel ignored his counsel and Sable found excuses to avoid him ever since his revelation about Annette.

Had Sable been spooked by the fact that he'd been married before? He failed to see how that affected their relationship. Sable had been married to someone else before they met, too, so if anything, it put them on more equal footing. But what else could account for the radio silence all week? It had been tough as hell to leave her at her apartment door without so much as a kiss goodnight after their day to-gether, but he'd forced himself to do so. He'd hoped that by respecting her boundaries, taking a break from the ever-present chemistry, he'd get her to trust him more.

But damned if he didn't feel more alienated from her than ever.

Closing the laptop with a muttered curse, Roman threw the plan to keep his distance out the window and charged out of the office into the studio. He needed to see Sable.

Now. Tonight.

When he reached the open workspace, however, his feet stalled as he took in the scene in front of him.

A slender model, who couldn't have been much older than fifteen, stood on the raised dais in front of a bank of windows. She wore a flame-red gown with a highly structured, asymmetrical design. One shoulder was bare, the other supported a decorative flourish that came to an exaggerated point beside her left ear. At the young woman's feet, Marcel and Sable sat together on the platform, heads bent together as they examined the dress's hem, comparing it to fab-ric swatches in Sable's hand.

Beside his tall, powerfully built brother, Sable looked absurdly feminine, with her soft curves en-cased in a pink cotton dress. Her wavy dark hair almost tipped onto Marcel's shoulder as she tilted her head to view a swatch from another angle. And damned if the sight of her so close to his sibling didn't make Roman feel short of breath.

It didn't matter that his brother was gay. Or that Roman cared about both of them. He just knew he wanted her close to him instead. Wanted it with a fierceness that put an edge in his voice.

"Sable."

They both turned toward him. He could feel his brother's scrutiny and guessed that Marcel saw more than Roman meant to reveal. But his focus was all for the woman beside his brother. Her color rose slightly at Roman's regard, and whatever she saw in his face caused her smile to falter. Emotion flickered in her hazel gaze. Annoyance? Awareness?

Too late, he remembered that his brother was unaware of their relationship. But there was no calling back Sable's name from Roman's lips now. He withdrew his phone to text his car service so there would be a ride waiting for them downstairs.

"I can finish up here," Marcel said, his attention shifting to Sable as he grabbed a tablet from the floor at the model's feet. "You've worked late every night this week, Sable. We can pick up with up my notes on accessories on Monday."

She frowned, her gaze darting between the two brothers before returning to the designer. "Are you sure? What about the fitting?"

"I'm almost done. And Cara can help me with the last dress." Marcel waved over one of the women at his drafting table who'd been looking at sketches.

The petite Black woman with long braids piled on her head rushed to his side and sank down beside him.

Sable passed her colleague the fabric swatches before she moved toward Roman, her pink skirt swishing with the subtle sway of her hips. Now he could read the frustration in her expression. A simmering emotion that bordered on anger.

"Yes?" She bit out the word while retrieving her handbag from a low couch.

Seeing her bend over the seat back, her curves pressing the fabric of her skirt, didn't do a thing to ease his need to have her next to him. His hands itched for the feel of her, for the chance to slide up her legs and explore the softness beneath her dress.

"I'd like to speak to you. Privately." His low voice was pure gravel, a direct result of the onslaught of hunger for her that he'd shoved to the back burner all week.

Hell, it had been longer than that, since he hadn't even touched her the last time they'd been together. The fascination with her only grew when he tried to ignore it.

Her jaw worked, revealing her resistance to how he'd called her away from her work, but she gave a short nod. He guessed she simply didn't want to discuss anything more with him while they had an audience. Now he had to hope she didn't bolt when they reached the street.

"Have a good weekend, you two," Marcel called over his shoulder, his tone so casual an observer might miss the undertone in his voice that let Roman know he hadn't missed the byplay.

That he'd expect answers about what was going on between his brother and his stylist intern.

Well, damn.

With their relationship effectively outed, Roman couldn't resist resting his hand at the small of Sable's back as they moved toward the elevator. He felt her tense, and nearly withdrew the touch.

But it was a good thing he didn't because then he would have missed her shiver. A swift, sweet undulation of her spine that called to the heat simmering hotter in his veins. He wasn't alone in this hunger.

Far from it.

When they entered the elevator, there was already an older woman inside, preventing conversation and giving Roman more time to work out what happened next. He hadn't formulated a plan ahead of time, which was unlike him. But he now knew this much—Sable might be avoiding him, but that didn't mean she wasn't aching with the same need he felt. And all at once, he hated that he'd left her alone all week. He could have fulfilled that need for both of them.

One way or another they needed to navigate a relationship, and the chemistry between them wasn't just going to disappear. He'd tried staying away from her enough times to know that for certain.

When they reached street level, he guided her out of the elevator and toward the waiting luxury SUV, a glossy black Escalade that he'd retained for the month. Seeing his intention, she halted outside the vehicle.

"I thought you wanted to talk," she said in her unhurried Southern cadence even though her eyes still snapped with frustration. She pouted, only making her full, bee-stung lips more irresistible.

"We can speak in the car." He let go of her to open the door, gesturing her inside.

She didn't move. "I was going to head home," she explained, wariness replacing her annoyance.

"Haven't you avoided me long enough?" He hooked his hand over the top of the door, prepared to debate this for the chance to spend time with her. "The clock is ticking on those nine months, Sable. We've got a lot to work out, including how we're going to share parenting when you dodge my texts and don't return my calls."

She pursed her lips. "You only called one time," she shot back, though she seemed to let her guard down because she stepped inside the Escalade, sliding across the back seat. "And I knew I'd see you at work, so I didn't see the need to ring you."

He followed her into the vehicle, taking the seat beside her and closing the door. The driver was impassive behind the partition but pulled away from the curb almost immediately; Roman had texted him their destination earlier.

"Right. Because you've been so chatty when I see you at the studio," he reminded her dryly. "You wanted to keep our relationship private, and I tried to respect that—"

"Until today." Folding her arms, she flashed him a look.

"Until today," he agreed easily, hoping she understood why. "When you gave me no easy option for speaking to you without drawing attention to the fact that we know each other outside of work."

For a moment, she didn't answer. She looked out the window as they headed north. Away from the route that would have taken them to her home in Brooklyn.

"Where are we going?" She turned toward him again, her hazel eyes wide, her pulse thrumming rapidly at the base of her neck.

He wanted to stroke that spot. Lick it. Taste it.

But only if her staccato heartbeat was a sign of excitement. He hoped like hell it was.

"I want to feed you dinner," he explained, lifting the hand that rested in her lap and bringing it to his lips. She watched him with rapt attention, her lips parting slightly as he skimmed a kiss along the pulse in her wrist. "I happen to know you worked right through lunch today, so you need to eat now. I'd prefer to cook for you myself, but if you want to go somewhere else we can."

The car stopped for a red light, jolting them slightly, giving him an excuse to wrap his arm around her and pull her toward him. He could feel her breath shudder through her before she released it in a long sigh and nodded.

"Okay. I'll go home with you, Roman. Just for dinner, though."

His own tension eased a fraction at her words. He wanted her to stay well past dinner, but for now, having her with him was enough. He stroked a hand over the back of her dark hair and told himself to be grateful for small victories, even if it might kill him to leave her at her own door tonight without a kiss.

Nine

"Where did you learn to cook like that?" Sable asked an hour later, sipping herbal tea from a sleek white mug as she sat on the sofa in Roman's temporary apartment.

They'd finished the frittata he'd whipped up in a flash after arriving, and she'd been more than a little impressed at his efficiency in the kitchen. She'd tried to help—before and after the meal—but he'd had his own cooking rhythm and insisted he wanted her to relax. Even now, he made short work of loading the dishwasher since he'd cleaned up after himself as he cooked.

Her gaze followed him as he moved around the kitchen with a red dish towel slung over the shoulder of his white dress shirt. The strong, shadowed jaw and hint of olive skin at the base of his throat where his collar remained unbuttoned called to her fingers to stroke him there.

"Marcel and I spent a lot of time with our grand-parents while we were growing up. My grandfather made his own fortune, and the equity firm I now oversee is his life's work." He started the dishwasher and then shut off the recessed lights in the kitchen, leaving on two pendants over the breakfast bar. "But my grandmother never lost her connection to sim-pler things, and she insisted Marcel and I learn how to prepare all her favorite dishes. Mostly traditional Lebanese dishes, but the frittata was something she liked to make for breakfast."

He joined her in the living room, taking a seat on the couch beside her. Feeling his heat so close viv-idly reminded her of what had happened between them the last time they'd shared this couch. She felt herself blush and ducked her head toward her ginger tea to hide her face. Knowing she should leave once she finished her drink.

But it had been too long since they'd touched each other. Longer still since they'd indulged an even deeper urge. Right now, she felt very aware of every week without him. Pulling her thoughts from the physical, she refocused on Roman's words to ground herself while she recovered her defenses. She knew his parents were celebrated academics who traveled extensively, but she hadn't realized that they'd left Roman and Marcel with their grandparents.

"I don't think your brother has many positive memories of your grandparents," she observed carefully, remembering a cutting comment Marcel had made about his judgmental grandfather in particular.

"With good reason." Roman's dark eyes veered to hers, his tone dust-dry. "Our parents were supportive when Marcel came out as gay at sixteen, but our paternal grandparents were...not. Their behavior drove a wedge into the family that never healed."

That was the impression she'd gotten. Only it was much worse than Roman made it sound. It wasn't her business. And yet, she felt a surge of loyalty for Marcel. She respected his talent and applauded his tireless humanitarian efforts for marginalized people. How dare his own family withdraw love and support from him during such a vulnerable moment in his life?

"Yet you remained close to them in spite of that?" Tensing, she set the mug of ginger tea aside. "Became your grandfather's protégé?"

"I wouldn't categorize the relationship as close, but I also didn't slash them out of my life. They'll never learn tolerance, let alone acceptance, if they're surrounded solely by people who think like they do."

She recognized some validity in his point, but she still didn't like thinking of Roman benefiting from the same family that had shunned Marcel.

Roman shifted on the couch beside her so that he could see her more fully. "Plus, as tempting as it might be to cut all ties with people who hurt my brother, that would have meant seeing our birthright sold off to strangers. Not just mine, but *his*, too. I wouldn't have minded for my own sake, but I'd be damned if I'd see Marcel wounded emotionally and then robbed financially, too." His scowl deepened for a moment before he let out a breath. "He deserved better than that. The stability of the equity firm gave us the capital we needed to build Zayn Designs. You see his talent. He deserves all the help I can give him."

Hearing the obvious pride in his voice soothed some of her ruffled defensiveness. "He's brilliant. Sometimes I have to pinch myself that I get to work so closely with someone who is destined to become a giant in the fashion industry."

"He will be. But first and foremost, he's my brother, and I need to tell him about the baby. Especially after the way we left together this afternoon." Roman's arm stretched along the back of the sofa so that he could twine his fingers in the ends of her hair. A gentle but potent gesture for the awareness it stirred. "I'm not going to deny that I like the idea of people knowing that you're carrying my child."

She met his dark gaze as she heard the hint of possessiveness in his voice. It shouldn't make her senses sizzle like that if they weren't going to have a relationship beyond shared parenting. But that didn't stop the desire from knotting in her belly, or keep her scalp from tingling as he smoothed a lock of hair between his fingers.

"I'm aware that we're reaching the point where I said we could start making plans." She sounded breathless and uncertain, but it was only because his touch made her ache for something she shouldn't want. Forcing herself to take a long breath in an attempt to relax herself, she continued with new steadiness. "The more I read about miscarriages at twelve weeks, the more reassured I am that we've already heard the heartbeat. It's a good sign I never had the first time I was pregnant. Should we tell your brother about the baby together?"

"I think his first reaction will be anger with me, so it might be best for me to speak to him alone until he moves past that." He searched her face, as if making sure she was okay with what he was suggesting. "I'll leave it to you to arrange for a less demanding work schedule."

She wanted to argue with him, to insist she could

maintain her workload in order to squeeze all the joy out of what would most likely be her final days in a field she loved. But she knew he only wanted to do what was best for the baby, and so did she. Which meant safeguarding her energy and her health. No doubt she'd been putting in long hours for months, and she needed to be better about respecting her body's limitations.

"All right. That sounds fair," she agreed after a moment, sitting forward on the couch to pick up the mug of tea again.

Her hair fell from his grasp as she leaned forward, breaking their connection.

"Thank you. This is good progress." His strong jaw flexed and relaxed over and over again in the pause afterward, until he finally went on. "Have you given any more thought to moving in with me once I secure an apartment in New York?"

She swallowed hard against the indecision that welled inside her. "Roman—"

He plowed right over the rest of her words, laying out his case. "I've already looked at some spaces, and have a few four-bedrooms in mind that might work well. There's one available in this building, but I wasn't sure how you felt about being that close to my parents once they return to town."

"Four bedrooms?" She couldn't even imagine what something like that cost in Manhattan. The building they were in was one of the most expensive in the city.

"We'd need a third for a nursery, and I thought a fourth would be wise so that we'd have an option for live-in help."

She was already shaking her head at the thought of residing in such close proximity to Roman. Just seeing him this evening felt fraught with tension as she battled her own urges. What would it be like to see him daily, in a private, intimate setting like a home where he might walk around the house without a shirt on?

Roman frowned, stroking along her arm. "Don't dismiss the idea until we see what it's like to have a newborn. You might be glad for a part-time nanny—"

"No." She shook her head more, pulling herself to her feet with the need to excise the jittery, anxious energy running through her. "I'm not arguing about the idea of live-in help. I'm saying no to living together. It won't work, Roman."

She took a lap around the windows of the curved great room, staying close to the perimeter where she could look out at the view of the city instead of the compelling man on the sofa. Her heels tapped softly over the hardwood.

She felt Roman's gaze follow her.

"It won't work to be in the same physical space as our child, so that there are at least two of us to answer the baby's needs, if not three? It's an exhausting business for the first year, Sable. This way we wouldn't be shuttling the baby around the city. Think how much safer and healthier it is for the child to be in one place." He hadn't moved from his spot on the sofa, giving her space to process what he was saying.

"You make it sound so reasonable. So easy." She reached the dining table in her pacing route and paused to look at him, his strong profile backlit by the skyline view behind him. "But since I could never afford my share of that lifestyle, I wouldn't feel at home—"

"You're bringing a child into the world. I think that more than evens out what we're offering." The deep sound of sincerity in his voice exerted a magnetic pull on her, drawing her inexorably toward this man.

"A child you never asked for or expected," she reminded him, folding her arms to try and shield herself from that pull.

"Neither did you, but here we are, and we both want the same thing. To be a part of this baby's life. To know the joys of being a parent." He rose to his feet, and her heart thudded harder with each footstep he took toward her. He stopped mere inches from her, his fingers reaching up to stroke over her cheek. "I told you about losing my wife. I thought the chance to be a father died with her since I'll never marry again."

Sable's breath caught sharply at the stark admission of his love for another woman. But she stifled the gasp, biting her lip to hold it back while his thumb caressed the soft place under her chin. When he spoke again, his voice was as persuasive as that touch.

"You're giving me something far more precious than any piece of real estate."

Despite all her efforts to reinforce her defenses around this man, Sable felt them melt into a puddle. Or maybe she was the one doing the melting. Everything inside her went soft and warm under the combined spell of his words and his light stroke over her skin.

"I never thought about it that way." Was it crazy of her to consider it when the need for him overwhelmed everything else? "Can I let you know at the ultrasound appointment? When I'm not so—"

She should make the decision when she was clearheaded. When she wasn't anticipating the feel of Roman's mouth on hers. The ultrasound was just three days away. Time enough for her to commit to where to go next.

His silken caress paused as he tilted her chin up to look at her. "When you're not so what?"

They were standing close enough now that each

time she dragged in a breath, her breasts grazed his chest. The feel of him, hot and solid against her, tantalized her.

"When I'm not under the influence of your touch? Of your hands that I want all over me?" She blurted the truth in a rush.

She'd thought he might kiss her then, crush his lips to hers and end this conversation that had her hormones and emotions swinging wildly. But he only tipped his forehead to hers, wrapping his hand around the back of her neck to encourage her gaze.

His eyes were so dark she could hardly see the brown ring around the rims.

"Okay. But keep in mind that we've already tried staying apart, Sable. We've done that, and it's only brought us right here, breathing each other in, dying to tear each other's clothes off so I can get inside you."

Roman watched Sable, half expecting her to contradict him.

He'd told her what he wanted, after recognizing all her cues that suggested she hungered for the same thing.

But pointing out that they both wanted this was a double-edged sword. For reasons he didn't fully comprehend, she had been avoiding the physical attraction. Even when the need was a red flush in her cheeks, a pulse throbbing double time at the base of her throat, and the rocking of her hips toward his, she was hesitant.

So he held himself very still, watching while her hazel eyes smoked with awareness. Her gaze traveled over him as if she was already imagining him without the barrier of clothing. Heat streaked up his spine.

"Last time we were here," he reminded her, still hoping to draw words from her that would give them both what they craved, "you wondered if intimacy would make it difficult to be objective about what happens next. Do you remember?"

"I do. I still don't have an answer to that." There was a husky quality to her voice that turned him inside out, even as he feared she would retreat from him again.

"All the more reason I need to know what you want to happen tonight." He was already strung tight, and the conversation made it worse. "Should I touch you, so we both feel better? Or take you home now in the hope of…" he ground his teeth in frustration, before forcing himself to finish the thought "…objectivity?"

Her lashes lowered, shutting him out while she seemed to weigh his words. He steeled himself for her answer. For another night without her in his bed.

When she peered up at him again, a determined glint in her eyes told him she'd made her decision.

"I want to stay." She licked her lips, then hauled in a deep breath before admitting in a lower voice, "I need you."

The words leveled him.

No, *she* leveled him.

Right then, he vowed to do everything in his power to make sure she didn't regret sharing that moment of vulnerability. Because damn, hearing the raw truth fed something inside him that he hadn't even realized was starved to hear it.

He wrapped his hands around her waist, pulling her close so her soft curves molded to him. Something about her smelled lemony and sweet. Her hair, maybe. Or her skin. He wanted that fragrance all over him.

"I need you, too," he assured her, stroking up her back to find the zipper of her pink crepe dress. "I've dreamed about touching you every night since that first time." Lowering the zipper, he parted the fabric slowly while he looked into her eyes. "Every. Single. Night."

A shiver trembled through her as the material began to slip off her shoulders.

"My skin—all of me—is so sensitive now." Her lashes fluttered against her cheek. "Just having the dress brush against my body teases me."

Head thrown back, lips parted, she looked like a fantasy with her dress ready to slide off her exquisite curves, glossy dark hair spilling down her back. But with the city lights flooding through the floor-to-ceiling windows, he felt exposed. He wasn't willing to share the sight of this incredible woman with anyone who happened to glance into the apartment's living room.

"I'm going to take care of that. Come with me." Not giving her a chance to answer, he lifted her higher against him, so her feet dangled a few inches from the floor.

He kissed her as he carried her through the apartment to the guest bedroom he'd claimed as his own. The blinds were already lowered, the only light coming from a high-tech chandelier that he dialed to the lowest setting as he set Sable on her feet, never breaking the kiss.

Her fingers worked the buttons of his shirt while he walked her backward toward the low platform bed that dominated the space. He tugged her already loosened dress down and off her body, catching the slippery pink crepe in one hand as she stepped out of it. He draped it over a tan leather chaise that served as the room's only other furniture, then peeled his shirt off the rest of the way. He could see that her gaze was avid even in the half-light, following his every movement.

It felt like forever since he'd touched her, and he couldn't wait another second. Flicking open the clasp of the pink satin bra that hugged her breasts, he took the soft weights in his hands, bringing each to his mouth in turn to kiss, lick and suck. Her back arched, fingers combing restlessly through his hair, holding him where she needed him as her hungry moans fueled a fire already scorching him.

"Please, please, please," she chanted, hips rocking so they pressed tighter to his.

Damn near blinding him with lust.

He hooked a finger in her pink satin panties, dragging them down and off her hips until she was fully naked. It was a sexy vision he knew he would replay often in his mind. But right now, he needed to make her feel good, to take the edge off all the hunger that had mounted over these last weeks.

Lowering himself to sit on the edge of the mattress, he drew Sable down on top of him so she straddled his hips. With a gasp, she rocked against him while he withdrew his wallet from his pants to retrieve the condom he kept there. She stilled his hand before he could open it, however.

"I'm clean," she whispered against his ear. "And already pregnant."

The thought of touching her that way—with zero barrier between them—took hold fast, creating a sharp hunger for something he would have never allowed himself to consider in other circumstances.

"I'm clean, too. You're the only woman I've been with since I was last tested." And then, of course, they'd used a condom.

Even though it hadn't protected her from getting pregnant.

"It's up to you." She let go of his hand, allowing him to decide whether or not to skip the protection. "But I wanted you to know I'm okay with not using anything."

Dropping the condom on the bed, he moved his hand to his fly. She joined her efforts to his, and they freed him a moment later, her fingers circling him. Stroking him.

Just that light touch had him seeing stars every time he blinked. Or maybe it was knowing that he was going to be inside her with nothing to dull the sensation of all that feminine heat.

Gripping her thighs, he lifted her so she was poised over him. Then he lowered her slowly, easing his way inside her until they both groaned at the contact.

She clamped her legs tight around his waist, holding him there while she pressed herself close against him. He licked a path up her neck, the lemon scent of her skin intensifying with the heat of his kiss. She shuddered, the roll of her hips reminding him of her new, heightened sensitivity. Testing that sensitivity, he molded a breast in his hand, running his thumb back and forth over the taut peak. When her breath caught, he transferred his lips to her nipple, drawing it into his mouth. He used his thumb to trace her feminine folds, circling the tight bud between her legs.

She arched her back so hard he almost stopped, but then the tremors swept through her, her sex pulsing around him with lush squeezes. It would have been so easy to let her release spur his. But he helped her ride out the sensation, giving her a moment to recover herself before he flipped her underneath him.

She blinked up at him with dazed, passion-filled eyes, her bee-stung lips fuller than ever. Hunger for her surged all over again, the need to claim her a fierce mandate, as if it were written in his DNA.

Holding her hips, he buried himself deep inside her. Over and over. Color rose in her cheeks, and her mouth worked soundlessly before she bit her lower lip. Roman quickly moved to kiss her, gently nipping and sucking on the fullness of her lower lip.

Her fingernails sank into his shoulders, and something about that light sting, as primitive a claim as his own, was what sent him over the edge. The force of his body's response was overpowering, and his hold on her tightened. He couldn't get close enough, and he would have sworn in that moment she felt the same way, with her limbs wound around his neck and his waist, her breasts molded to his chest.

Their shouts mingled, breaths huffing harshly in sync.

His heart hammered in his chest like it needed out, but his senses slowly returned. Closing his eyes, he rolled to his side, bringing Sable with him. He tucked her close to his chest and drew a corner of the lightweight duvet over her, covering her from shoulder to knee. As their pulses slowed, he brushed her dark hair from her face, combing lightly through the strands with his fingers.

She made a satisfied hum in her throat, a sound he wasn't even sure she was aware of as she cuddled closer. Something about that soft note of contentment crawled into his consciousness, taunting him with all he could never give her.

Did it matter that he wanted to provide for their child and give her a home when he couldn't offer her the love and commitment he'd shared with his wife? Four bedrooms in one of the city's most coveted apartments didn't seem like much compared to the daily joys of a partner who could offer her love and commitment.

If he couldn't give her that, was it even fair of him to ask her to move in with him?

A chill crept over him at the thought that he was being selfish to try to convince her to stay in New

York for his convenience. So that he could know his child and help to raise him or her.

He hated to think what she would be missing out on. Especially since she hadn't been as fortunate as him in her first marriage. She hadn't known the kind of deep and abiding love he'd shared with Annette, so it would be all the more cruel of him to expect her to live with him when he knew he couldn't give her those things.

Her soft, even breaths slowed, falling into the cadence of sleep. And Roman was grateful that she wasn't awake to witness the churn of emotions he wrestled with now. Because whether or not it was fair of him to ask her to move in with him, he still wanted to. Needed to have his child and heir in close proximity.

His only hope was that Sable savored her independence as much as he needed his. Maybe then, they could live together and raise a child together without anyone getting hurt.

Any other alternative was unacceptable. He'd already lost too much to lay his heart on the line again.

Ten

Standing in front of her bedroom closet two days later, Sable still had no idea whether she should say yes to moving in with Roman or not. She stared at the calendar on her phone, where a reminder had just popped up about the twelve-week ultrasound appointment scheduled for the next day. She'd told Roman she'd get back to him with an answer by then, but she was still just as confused as ever.

Maybe more so since the unforgettable night she'd spent in his bed.

With a sigh, she tugged a few Zayn Designs sample dresses from the closet and began to pull the protective bags off the hangers. She was preparing for an impromptu social media photo shoot with her housemates. Blair and Tana had agreed to the idea as a creative group project, and Sable hoped it would give her an opportunity to tell her friends the news that she needed to move out of the house.

Was she giving up on her dream of being a celebrity stylist too easily if she opted to go back home to Baton Rouge to have her baby? Or was it a smart move to relocate where she would have a more affordable lifestyle as well as the love and support of her family during a time of tremendous change? It might be easier to decide if her feelings for Roman weren't so complicated. But the more time they spent together, the more she found to like about him.

His obvious concern for the baby was extremely compelling, of course. But there were other things that called to her, like the way he put her in charge of where she wanted their relationship to go, never taking advantage of her obvious attraction to him. She liked that he championed her career dreams, reminding her of her goals outside of motherhood. As much as she craved the chance to be a parent, she recognized that her yearning was tangled up with her past. It was so difficult not to fear for this pregnancy every moment of every day. She was grateful to Roman for challenging her to look beyond this pregnancy to ensure she put a value on her work.

The notes of an electric violin solo grew louder outside her bedroom door, warning her that music lover Tana was approaching.

"You're next in the makeup chair," Tana called as she reached the fourth floor of their Brooklyn brownstone. A moment later, the petite actress stepped across Sable's threshold dressed in black booty shorts and a worn T-shirt with a rainbow outlined in rhinestones. She wore red clip-in braids today, but her understated makeup showed off flawless skin. "Blair already did my face, but I drew the line at letting her touch my hair. Do you mind if I leave my braids in for the photo?"

"Of course not." Standing, Sable passed her the hangers with Marcel's dresses before grabbing a pair of silver sandals for herself. "I like the idea of a photo of us all because we'd each look so different in the clothes."

Tana arched an eyebrow at her before heading toward the door to go downstairs. "So it's fine that Blair will look like a *Vogue* cover while I rock more of a 'Tinker Bell on an acid trip' vibe?"

Following Tana to the parlor, Sable laughed, grateful for the distraction from her worries about what to tell Roman and where to raise her baby. "Personally, I'd call it music festival glam. But that's the beauty of using real people in social media images for the brand. Followers with all different aesthetics can see how the clothes could work for them."

They reached the parlor floor where Blair had two fishing tackle boxes open on a wooden sideboard between two windows overlooking the backyard. She had dragged one of the living room chairs to the window for better light. Blair was currently studying what looked like smudges of lipstick in various colors on the backs of her hands.

"Cool. But don't stop there," Tana cautioned as she passed a cream-colored sheath dress to Blair. "You need more diversity in the Zayn Designs feed. You've done a good job with skin tones, but what about showcasing more kinds of figures? And people who are differently abled?"

"You're right." Sable appreciated the feedback and tapped a note into her phone as she sat in the makeup chair by the window. "That's important to Marcel, too. I'll remind him we need samples in more sizes. And thank you both for doing this."

"Are you kidding?" Blair said, digging in one of the tackle boxes and pulling out a sleek black case containing a compact. "This is like grown-up playtime for me."

"Even though you do this every day for work?" Sable asked, curious to know more about her friends before life pulled them apart.

Blair nodded as she swirled a brush through the

powder inside the compact and then patted it onto Sable's cheek. "I got into makeup because I always liked sprucing up my friends and making them feel pretty. But in the last few years, pursuing it as a profession, I don't have as many opportunities to do faces just for fun. It's nice not to have an exacting client breathing down my neck telling me to erase someone's freckles or fill in scars."

While Sable mused over that, Tana pulled her T-shirt off and slid one of the Zayn slip dresses over her head. As she wiggled the silk into place, she strode closer. "Is Lucas Deschamps one of those exacting bosses?"

Blair's mouth pulled into a frown before she answered, "Lucas and I have very different visions. He believes makeup should be like fashion, and you should introduce a new look each season with all of the brand supporting the look. I happen to like faces that tell a story, and think sometimes makeup should take a back seat to the face."

Sable and Tana exchanged a look at their friend's uncharacteristically grim tone.

"Maybe there's a middle ground in there somewhere," Tana suggested carefully before she pirouetted in her cream-colored slip dress. "And this is the most gorgeous outfit I've ever worn, by the way. You must get along well with your boss, Sable, for him to trust you with all these great clothes."

Blair glanced up from an eye shadow palette. "Was that your boss who picked you up outside the brownstone two weeks ago? I saw you get into an SUV with a really hot guy wearing shades that first day I toured the house with Cybil."

"A hot guy?" Tana leaned a hip on the makeup table. "Do tell."

This was it. The time had come to tell them about Roman and the baby. Nerves knocked around inside her, but she pressed ahead.

"That wasn't the designer. That was Roman Zayn, Marcel's brother." She felt her cheeks warm for no good reason. She wasn't embarrassed by their relationship. "He handles the business end of the fashion house."

"But has he handled *you*?" Tana asked while Blair squealed with delight at the question.

Sable struggled to find the right way to admit their relationship without making it sound completely inappropriate. "Any and all handling was mutual."

Blair stopped working on Sable's face to gape at her. "I knew there was a hot vibe there when I saw you two together. I knew it."

"Is he the reason for the prenatal vitamins you left in the kitchen cupboard?" Tana pressed.

"Oh no." Sable dropped her head into her hands. "Did I honestly do that?"

So much for trying to find a tactful way to share

the news. Clearly her pregnancy brain was broadcasting the news for her without her knowing.

"Seriously?" Blair knelt in front of her, forehead knit in concern as she rested a hand on Sable's knee. "Are you really…expecting?"

Deep breath. Her life would change forever once she said the words.

"Yes. I'm twelve weeks along. And it's a good thing. It's just that it was totally unexpected and I'm having to make a lot of decisions about what to do next." She'd done a half-hearted search for apartments in Baton Rouge, but she couldn't see herself back there, raising her baby alone while her ex-husband lived nearby with his new wife and growing family.

Blair sat on her heels, brushing aside her blond ponytail. "What kinds of decisions? Can we help?"

Briefly, she outlined the pros and cons of Roman's proposal that she move in with him versus returning to Louisiana. The biggest drawback of life in Baton Rouge, of course, would be watching her career dreams go up in smoke.

Tana twirled one of her red clip-in braids around her finger. "Why wouldn't you just stay here? I like babies." She glanced over at Blair. "Chances are good that Blair likes babies."

Blair nodded vigorously in the affirmative at this statement. "We'll help you. That way you can finish your internship, and go back to work when you're ready. On your own terms."

Touched beyond measure at their kindness, Sable blinked away happy tears at the vision of remaining in the apartment. "As amazing as that sounds, I'm pretty sure Cybil will want me to leave the apartment if I'm not actively pursuing a career in one of the creative fields—"

"But you are," Tana argued, folding her arms, and speaking with a new fierceness. "The whole idea behind this apartment house was to support single women trying to get ahead in artistic careers. Well, guess what? Pregnancy is part of a woman's life, and we're going to support you through that until you can return to your work. If Cybil doesn't like that, she can kick all of us to the curb."

Tana's impassioned speech was such a surprise there was a moment of silence afterward. But Blair recovered first, giving it a slow clap that turned into full-fledged cheers and wolf whistles that made Tana roll her eyes.

As for Sable, she was so overcome by the generosity of her new friends that she hardly knew what to say.

"Thank you," she finally said, recovering her voice even though there was still a lump in her throat. "Without a doubt, that's the coolest, sweetest offer anyone has ever made me." She stood up and surprised Tana with a hug. Then, before she could offer one to Blair, Blair joined them for a group hug.

The gift of friends having her back—very literally at the moment—provided her a much-needed confidence boost.

"Cybil won't object to this, by the way," Blair said as they broke apart. "She might use it as publicity when she goes to search for the next round of candidates when we move out—a way to show off girl power in action—but she wouldn't try to kick you out of the building just because you're pregnant."

"You don't think so?" Sable hadn't reread all the fine print on the contract she'd signed when she moved in, but had just assumed it would be a huge imposition on the other women in the house to have a baby take up residence.

But Tana and Blair seemed adamant. Excited, even.

"Not a chance." Blair gestured to the makeup chair, wordlessly inviting Sable to sit back down. "We spoke for a long time the day she gave me the tour of the house, and she reminisced about her days of living in the Barbizon Hotel. She made the closest friendships of her life there, and that's what she hoped to foster here, too. She'll think this is cool."

"What will Lucas think?" Tana pondered aloud, in a laughably obvious ploy to get a rise out of Blair.

Blair took the bait without a second thought. "Like

everything else in life, he'll probably think he could do it better, faster and more efficiently," she snapped. "But clearly, no one cares what he thinks."

"Clearly." Tana winked at Sable before her expression turned serious. "The bigger question is what Roman will say once he knows he's lost his leverage to get you to move in with him."

Leverage?

Her friend's more cynical view of Roman's motives troubled her. Sable had viewed his offer as generous. But even he had reminded her that by having his child, she was bringing more to the equation than he was. Was it possible that he was trying to use his wealth and power to maneuver her into a position that suited him best?

Certainly. But she couldn't fault him when he didn't have to make the offer to begin with. He could have simply sent her child support and walked away. She fully believed that he wanted to be a part of this baby's life.

And a small part of her even felt a twinge of guilt that he wouldn't have as much time with their infant if she accepted the offer to remain in the brownstone. But bottom line, she needed to make a decision that wasn't just good for the baby, but for herself, too.

"I don't know what Roman will say," Sable finally mused aloud, after Tana had moved off to set up the backdrop for the group photo.

Blair heard her, though, and paused between coats of mascara to look into Sable's eyes.

"If he's a good man, he'll put the mother of his child first," Blair told her firmly. "He'll understand that you need to live where you're most comfortable."

Sable agreed in theory. But she still felt a knot in her chest at the thought of telling Roman her potential new plan. Because no matter how much sense it made, she recognized how the separation from his baby would hurt him.

She would be lying if she pretended that it wouldn't affect her, too. But that was what happened when you developed feelings for someone—their pain was yours.

And that was when she understood the truth. Despite her best intentions, she was falling for Roman. Hard. What a sad, hurtful moment to realize how close she was to loving a man who could never return those feelings.

Seated in the courtyard of a vacant Broome Street storefront the next day, Roman stole a glance at his watch to make sure he budgeted himself enough time to get uptown for Sable's ultrasound appointment. His brother and their Realtor were still inside the building, reviewing the space and making notes on how it could work for a Zayn Designs flagship store.

Roman had set up the showing since he'd been

tracking Manhattan real estate closely over the last two weeks, and he'd seen the SoHo location come on the market the night before. And while he absolutely wanted to secure a prime storefront for Zayn Designs, his motive might have also been driven by a need to get back in his brother's good graces after Marcel's reaction to the news that Sable was expecting Roman's baby.

Scrolling through his phone while he waited for Marcel to finish up, Roman heard Marcel's damning words in his head.

Of all the women in this city, you had to take up with the best stylist I have? A woman who has single-handedly tripled the Zayn social media outreach when that wasn't even in her job description?

Roman hadn't been aware of the impact she'd had on the brand. Not that it would have made a difference since his attraction to Sable wasn't something he could have ignored. But Marcel had taken it as a personal affront that Roman had initiated a relationship with someone in their employ. Even worse, Marcel had anticipated what a baby would mean for Sable's hours on the job, even though Roman hadn't asked him to consider lightening her schedule. Marcel had warned Roman that he would need Sable to meet her work obligations.

The argument had only grown more heated from there. Thankfully, Sable had been scheduled for a job off-site on a two-day shoot with an Italian magazine spotlighting new American designers, so she hadn't been subjected to the tension in the Zayn studio.

"Roman." Marcel stepped out into the courtyard through the back door of the vacant shop. Hands shoved in the pockets of black jeans, he stopped just outside the double doors, crossing one loafer in front of the other as he leaned against the doorframe. "The Realtor asked us to lock up when we leave. He had another appointment. I know you do, too."

A hint of bitterness shaded Marcel's words at the reference to the ultrasound appointment.

Leaning back in his chair, Roman observed his brother warily. He had no wish to revisit the arguments of the day before. "What do you think of the space?"

"It's ideal. I'm sure it will get snapped up in a hurry, probably for the full asking price." Marcel's eye roamed over the courtyard surrounded by low brick walls. The surrounding buildings were taller with even higher fences, but that didn't detract from the patch of open sky overhead.

"We can at least make an offer. I'll text the Realtor to get the ball rolling." Roman thumbed in a number on his phone and hit Send.

Marcel nodded his approval, but continued in a stern tone. "I want you to know that I'm going to offer Sable the apartment at the studio."

Roman's gaze flew to his brother's. "What?"

He had to have misheard. Misunderstood. Surely
Marcel wouldn't undermine Roman's efforts to build
a relationship with his child by enticing Sable into
an alternative housing situation.

"I don't use that apartment very often, so it won't
be an inconvenience to have her there. And I can't
abide the possibility that she'd leave New York before the internship ends just because she can't afford
to stay. She's too valuable to me and to the brand."

Resentment burst inside Roman like a firework.
"Screw the brand, Marcel. Don't you think she's far
more valuable to me as the mother of my child?"

His brother arched an eyebrow. "If that's the case,
I would think you'd be all the more grateful for the
chance to keep her in the city instead of watching
her jet off a thousand miles away to raise your baby
without you."

Just the thought of that happening made him ill.
Would she really consider such a drastic move simply to avoid living with him? He remembered how
she'd felt in his arms three nights ago, how she'd
trusted him with her body and her pleasure. Surely
he hadn't been alone in the sense that they were right
together? They didn't need to tangle up their emotions when they had a smart plan that was mutually
beneficial for their future.

"Sable isn't going to leave New York." He'd been

confident she'd see the wisdom of living together. And she was supposed to give him an answer this afternoon at the appointment. "She's going to move in with me because she wants to do what's best for our child."

"What about what's best for her?" Marcel gave him a narrow look. "She was already married to one selfish jackass who couldn't look beyond his own needs to ensure her happiness. She doesn't need another."

Roman hung onto his temper with both hands, unwilling to cross swords with his brother again. "How is it selfish to offer her a real home here, with space for her and her child, and a man by her side who's as invested in caring for the baby as she would be?"

"Wealth doesn't solve every problem, Roman. Trust me when I tell you that it doesn't even begin to make up for a lack of love." The words lingered in the air between them, so thick with old hurts it became obvious that there was more on Marcel's mind than just concern for Sable.

Was this his brother's way of telling him that he resented Roman's continued dealings with their grandfather? The thought rocked him, forcing him to question how he'd spent the last decade.

"Are you suggesting I should have walked away from Zayn Equity? Even when that income has financed every aspect of the fashion house?" A helicopter flew over the building, casting a brief shadow on them both.

Marcel blew out a long breath. "Forget it."

"I damned well won't." Roman shot to his feet, needing answers. "If I'd known you viewed my work with the equity firm as disloyal to you for even a second, I would have never taken a role there. And if you still do, I'll submit my resignation this afternoon."

Marcel studied him for a moment. Then, perhaps recognizing that Roman meant every word, he shook his head. "No. I might have seen it that way a few times over the years on days Granddad has been particularly brutal in his disregard for me. But I understand your reasons, and appreciate that your work has ensured we had the capital to start Zayn Designs."

"Yet you don't believe I have Sable's best interests at heart." Roman knew without looking at his watch that he needed to leave now if he wanted to make it to the ultrasound appointment on time.

He pulled open the door to return to the storefront so they could lock up behind them.

Marcel followed him inside before he spoke again. "I think you're too concerned with not having your heart broken again to recognize that you're going to push away an incredible woman if you don't get your act together."

Marcel had it all wrong. It wasn't concern for his heart that kept Roman from Sable, but his promise to Annette. Bottom line, that didn't make a difference when the outcome was still that Roman kept Sable at arm's length.

They could kiss, touch and turn each other inside out with shared passion. They could even raise a child together. But none of that changed the truth that he'd promised his heart to another.

He just hoped it didn't push away Sable for good.

Eleven

As she lay on the exam table in the imaging room, Sable kept her eyes on the screen projecting a black-and-white image of their baby. A tech in purple scrubs rolled the transducer over Sable's belly, sometimes increasing the pressure to enhance the picture or take a particular measurement. Ten minutes into the scan, all the signs were normal, with the tech pointing out the developmental cues she was looking for as she worked.

Sable relaxed enough to glance over at Roman on the other side of the exam table, his gaze rapt as he watched the screen. She'd sensed tension in him today when they'd met in the outer office, but he had sidestepped her questions, insisting they could talk later.

As if she wasn't already nervous enough about telling him she was considering remaining in the Brooklyn brownstone with her friends. Certainly, he would understand. But she knew he would be disappointed because he seemed to genuinely want this baby as much as she did. His sense that this would be his only chance to be a parent was sure to give him a good relationship with the child. But it made it more difficult to distinguish his concern for his heir from his feelings for her.

As of now? She could only assume she didn't figure into his future in any role beyond mother of his child. And the sooner they both accepted as much, the easier it would be to forge a new relationship based on shared parental concerns instead of shared passion.

To support that goal, she really needed to end their physical relationship.

"How are you doing?" Roman asked, his gaze suddenly focused on her.

Even that simple concern made her heart flutter. Especially since it was accompanied by a warm squeeze of her hand. He stroked the backs of her knuckles with his thumb, and used his free hand to smooth her hair from her forehead.

And that quickly, his touch threatened her resolve. How much easier would it be to simply let him take charge of the housing? To rely on him to help her prepare for the new arrival, and to share in the care-giving? But she knew where that kind of relationship would lead. Right back to the feelings of worthlessness she'd battled when Jack had left her.

It was one thing to rely on a man who was supposed to love you. But Roman had been very clear that he wouldn't be that man.

"I'm fine," she assured him, even though she was far from it.

Even though she could already tell how deeply she would miss his touch. Their relationship had rushed forward with heated intensity, the pregnancy only adding to the bond. She ached at the thought of losing that connection, but the longer she let herself feel this way about him, the harder it would be to walk away. And she couldn't imagine how she'd ever know or trust his real motivation for having her in his life.

"I can't believe how much the baby is moving." His gaze briefly flicked back to the screen before returning to her, a hint of wonder in the dark depths of his eyes. "You don't feel that?"

She shook her head, smiling at the sight of the squirming little figure on the screen. "Not even a little. I think I read most first-time mothers don't feel the baby move until week sixteen or later."

"That's going to be an incredible moment for you when you do." He lowered his head to brush a kiss across her temple, voice dropping for her ears alone. "I hope I'm touching you when it happens."

A pleasurable shiver stole over her, quickly followed by a genuine chill as she remembered the conversation they needed to have after the appointment. The thought made it difficult to focus on the rest of the ultrasound, although she tuned in enough to savor the news that her baby was growing normally and continued to thrive, a blessing she could still barely believe was really happening.

Twenty minutes later, after putting back on the floral pencil skirt and red puff-sleeve blouse she'd worn for what she suspected would be the last time during her pregnancy, Sable accepted the arm Roman offered her as he accompanied her down the elevator and outside.

"How should we celebrate a successful and healthy twelve weeks?" he asked as they stepped out into the late-afternoon sunshine. "Dinner? Shopping for cribs? It's not too early to think about what you want in a nursery."

His enthusiasm for the baby pierced her heart. For a moment, she allowed herself to imagine what it would be like to share those milestones with Roman at her side. How different today would be if she could simply say yes. She could imagine Roman comparing car seat features with her by day, then delivering toe-curling orgasms by night. But commitment to their child—even when combined with commitment to her pleasure—wasn't the same as love for *her*.

And the sooner her traitorous body got the message, the better off she'd be.

"We're close to the park." She pointed toward the Seventy-Second Street entrance, remembering the cherry trees she'd used as a backdrop for some photos the month before. "Do you mind if we walk around a little? I've been cooped up indoors all day."

"Sure." He agreed easily enough, but she didn't miss the flash of wariness in his dark eyes before he escorted her across Fifth Avenue and into Central Park.

They made small talk for a few minutes, discussing what parts of the park they'd seen. Since Sable was new to New York City and Roman spent more of his time on the West Coast, they still had a lot to explore.

The Cherry Hill Fountain was in sight when she asked him about his home in Los Angeles. Even though she needed to break their romantic connection, she still wanted to know about Roman's family and his home since their child would undoubtedly spend time there. Without her.

Sable's heart squeezed.

"My place is in Malibu now, so I can be near the

water." He hooked his arm around her waist as they passed a group of schoolkids, all dressed in matching T-shirts, touring the park. "My grandparents lived in Anaheim when Marcel and I were growing up. Our parents had a little place in Westwood, close to the university, but we didn't spend much time there since they traveled so much."

"Malibu?" She didn't know her West Coast geography very well, but she had a vision of crashing surf and beautiful sunsets. How welcome would she be there once she told Roman that she didn't want to live together? Would he stop wooing her?

"It's a long way from the city—in miles and in mindset. I keep an apartment downtown in case I need to be in the office on back-to-back days, but for the most part, I work from home." He guided them toward a vacant bench near the fountain with its wide granite pool.

A group of joggers and a bicyclist swooped around the circular concourse, but other than that they were alone. A few couples and families played on Cherry Hill overlooking Bow Bridge and the Ramble. The view was so pretty and rural she could almost forget they were in uptown Manhattan.

But she couldn't afford to forget why they were here. She'd purposely chosen a public place to explain to him why they couldn't continue a romantic entanglement. She hoped the outdoor venue would serve as a reminder that she shouldn't kiss and touch him anymore.

"That sounds nice," she admitted as she took a seat on the wrought iron bench, musing on his life on the other side of the country. A life she'd never be a part of, even though her child would be.

"I hope you'll take advantage of it once you're ready to resume working." He sat close to her, his arm draped over the bench behind her back, his palm a warm weight on her shoulder. "It would be ideal for your work as a celebrity stylist since you'd have a couple of home bases you could work from."

His thoughtful concern for her future twisted in her chest, making it hard to breathe.

She needed to tell him about her new plans. Delaying would only make things more complicated. Would only put her heart at greater risk.

"That's kind of you to suggest," she began carefully, closing her eyes for a moment as she drew in a steadying breath. Then, she forced herself to meet his dark gaze. "But I've given it a lot of consideration, and I really think it's better that we keep our households separate."

In the aftermath of her declaration, the sounds of squealing children playing Frisbee and the rhythmic thump of a jogger's sneakers hitting the pavement seemed out of sync. Off-kilter. Roman stared at her, his forehead wrinkled as he took in the words.

His hand on her shoulder tensed. "Meaning you don't want to move into a shared apartment with me? Or are you still contemplating a return to Louisiana?"

Concern laced his voice. Tension. She needed to rip the Band-Aid off this painful conversation.

"My housemates offered to help me with the baby. They insist I can still live in the brownstone so I can finish my internship." She felt a burst of pride that her friends had extended the offer. She wasn't alone. She needed to remind herself of that as her heart ached over giving up moving in with Roman.

"And you would rather your friends care for our child when you're not around than me? The child's father?" He spoke with slow deliberateness that made her realize how very still he'd gone. Pain flashed in his eyes.

Empathy tugged at her, warning her this wouldn't be easy for him to accept.

"We'll still share custody of course—"

"Without question." The brusque words reminded her how much he wanted this child. The protective instinct ran deep for them both.

She shifted on the bench to face him, taking another approach. "But I need people around me to support *me*, Roman."

"And you think I wouldn't do that?" He spread

his arms wide, a gesture that somehow emphasized how ludicrous he found the suggestion.

"I'm sure you would try, but I need more than support, okay?" She hadn't wanted to spell it out so baldly, afraid of how desperate it made her seem. But she knew he'd never give her what she needed most, and she was equally sure he understood that it wasn't within his capability to give. "If I don't have the love of my family to help me as a single parent, I at least need the love of friends."

"Love." His arms fell back to his sides, his shoulders drooping as if under an enormous weight.

And didn't that speak volumes about how hopeless it was for her to ever imagine him giving her that valuable commodity?

Her chest hurt. Her eyes stung. And her heart broke.

"It nearly killed me to realize that I married a man who chose me only because I checked the right boxes for the kind of life he wanted. And when I stopped checking an important box—the baby-making requirement—I was as disposable as yesterday's news." She'd fought back, though, and recovered a new life for herself.

She wouldn't sacrifice that now. For herself. And to model strength for her child.

"Please don't compare me to a man who couldn't appreciate you for all you have to offer, Sable." The anguish in his voice—in his eyes—was real. "I told you that you shouldn't shortchange your dreams. I would make sure you had the resources you need to return to your work. Hell, I just told you to come to Malibu once you're ready—"

"And I'm so grateful for that. You were the one who made me see that I couldn't go back to Baton Rouge just because I craved the love of my family during a challenging time. You helped me see the consequences of compromising too much of myself, and I can't thank you enough for making me see that." She was a stronger woman for knowing him.

His hand clenched and unclenched where it rested on his knee, and his voice sounded hollow when he spoke again. "But that doesn't mean you want to live with me. Even knowing we'll both see our child less this way."

Her chest ached at the thought, a heavy sorrow weighing her down that they couldn't be the family she'd dreamed of having. But she was doing the best she could.

She spoke a last, futile hope out loud before she could think better of it. "If I thought there was any chance that love might grow between us one day—"

At the dark look in his eyes, the rest of the words dried up. Her hopes withered along with them.

"My brother was right," he said finally, scrubbing a hand over his face. "Marcel said that wealth doesn't make up for a lack of love. Apparently, a portfolio is all I've got to offer anyone."

They must have walked out of the park soon afterward, but Sable didn't remember much from the rest of their time together. Roman had a car pick them up outside the park, and he saw her safely back to the brownstone where he said something about a contract that would formalize a custody arrangement.

When he dropped her off, she stared up at the apartment building that had once represented all her hopes and dreams of a new life. Now it would be the haven she would return to, when she brought her baby home from the hospital. Alone. Tears threatened as the image blurred in front of her eyes.

She didn't look back as she walked up the front steps. Not after the way Roman had shut down at the mention of love between them. His reaction had told her more clearly than any words that she'd been wise to break things off between them before she was irretrievably in love with him. Except, from the way hurt cracked her insides now, Sable knew she'd been too late.

She loved Roman.

And he'd all but admitted there wasn't a chance in hell he'd ever love her back.

Drained, Roman returned to his parents' vacant New York apartment for the last time to clear out his things, knowing he couldn't remain in Manhattan when Sable didn't want him in her life.

He called his Realtor to put his search for an apartment on hold since there was no rush to set up his place. He would still get something to facilitate seeing his child, of course, and living in the same city as Sable made the most sense. All that damn money gave him options. But he wouldn't be her unwelcome shadow for the next twenty-eight weeks, even though he already missed her.

And not just in his bed.

He already missed holding her hand. Hearing about her day. And he missed the chance to feel his child move in her belly, along with a whole host of moments he wouldn't get to be a part of now.

It had been five years and three months since he'd felt this empty and alone. A thought which had him opening his laptop at the kitchen counter, seeking a hidden file that he rarely let himself open.

Inside the file were old photos. Pictures of his life with Annette back when he'd been a different man. A better man, who had more to offer than a fat bank account.

He'd forgotten how blue her eyes were. Maybe because Sable's were hazel and that was the color he saw in his dreams now. Was that so wrong? So disloyal?

His vow to love Annette forever hadn't just been

some wishful youth's romantic thinking at her death-bed. He'd promised it to her in desperation, as part of a plea to convince her to stay strong in her heart surgery, as if he could animate her exhausted body with his own fierce will. Maybe it had been a youth's wishful thinking after all.

Scanning more photos, he paused on one from their trip to the Seychelles. He recognized the beach they'd visited on the north shore of Praslin Island—a long stretch of soft, blond sand and crystal-blue water. Annette was alone in the photo, laughing as she slung an arm around a palm tree. As he enlarged the image, the T-shirt she wore caught his eye, a simple white T-shirt with black block letters containing an Emily Dickinson quote: "That it will never come again is what makes life so sweet."

The words hit him like a freight train. Especially seeing them on the woman he loved who would be dead just nine months after the photo was taken.

Cursing, he shoved the photo away from him, unable to look at it. But memories flowed over him anyhow, moments he hadn't thought about in years.

He remembered her buying the shirt. He even remembered talking about why she liked the quote since, at the time, a new transplant hadn't even been on their radar. She'd been in great health, and she was the most vital, vibrant woman he'd ever met at the time they married.

Yet she was always aware of that quote, she'd told him. It was why she lived every day with so much love and joy. She knew life could be taken from her at any moment, and she refused to waste a second of the time she had.

Hot tears burned his eyes and his throat as he forced himself to open his laptop again and look at the image. To look at her, and really see her. Not just the woman he'd loved, but an inspirational figure. A woman who had deep, meaningful insight into life, insight he'd been unable to fully appreciate because he'd just mindlessly wanted that love and joy to last forever.

Shame washed over him like a rogue wave. Not for loving her—never that. But for not *listening* to her. For not honoring the gifts she'd tried to give him.

His whole universe shifted. Or maybe just his view of it changed. But in that moment he had startling clarity for what he had to do next. He had a lot of work to do, and life was too precious for him to waste another second in the narrow wasteland of his grief.

First and foremost, he would write a letter to his grandfather relinquishing his position as CEO of Zayn Equity. He'd read between the lines with his brother, and no matter what Marcel said, Roman could see that maintaining the connection to their grandfather's business hurt his brother. If they got disinherited, Roman would move around his assets and find a way to still finance Zayn Designs until it was operating firmly in the black.

He shot to his feet to retrieve his phone. On his way across the living room, he texted the Realtor again to sweeten the offer on the Broome Street storefront. One way or another, Marcel would have a good launchpad for the flagship store.

Full of hope and determination, Roman racked his brain for a way to show Sable he'd been wrong about what he had to offer her. There was more than wealth, damn it.

There had to be, since he'd have less of it at his disposal now that he was about to cut ties with the equity firm.

He wasn't sure how long he sat there, thinking and planning, but the dawn was approaching when he got a text from a number he didn't recognize.

This is Blair, Sable's roommate. I'm taking her to the hospital. She started bleeding—

The words blurred until he couldn't even see them. His brain hammered, not just with fear for his child, but for Sable, until a single thought drowned out all the rest.

He had to be at her side, no matter what.

Twelve

Sable felt cold everywhere.

Shivering under the bleach-scented blanket an emergency room nurse had given her, she listened as Blair explained her symptoms for the second time since they'd arrived. The first time had been to the admitting nurse. Now Blair repeated the story for an attending doctor who said he'd already called for an obstetrician. Sable had been assigned a room and a bed almost immediately, the hurried movement of the ER staffers telling her they took her condition seriously.

How could she be losing her baby when she'd just

seen it moving in an ultrasound twelve hours ago? After crying herself to sleep over the breakup with Roman, she'd awoken to cramps and bleeding a little after 3:00 a.m. She'd almost fainted when she realized what was happening, the trauma of it making her knees turn to jelly so that she stumbled against the sink and shouted for her friends.

Tana had called an Uber, insisting it would be faster than an ambulance. Then she'd personally directed the driver to the drop-off entrance while Blair held Sable's hand and told her everything would be okay.

Even though nothing was okay.

A minute or two after the attending physician stepped away from the exam room, a commotion sounded outside the door, and Sable hoped the specialist had arrived. As she pushed up in the bed, the door swung open to admit…

Roman.

Wrong though it might be, she couldn't help the rush of relief at seeing him. No one else knew how worried she'd been. She hadn't confided in Blair and Tana about the other miscarriage. In spite of all the hurt and heartache she felt with Roman, she knew without question he would understand. Empathize.

"I got here as fast as I could." Striding closer, he wove his way around a rolling table and dodged a scowling Tana.

"How did you know where to find me?"

"Your roommate texted me." He glanced at Blair, who was standing beside the bed. "Thank you."

He sat down at Sable's other side, dropping onto the bed, strong arms offering her a comfort she desperately needed.

She couldn't have possibly denied herself that consolation. She tipped her head against his solid, warm chest, knowing he was feeling the same wrenching sense of loss that had devastated her ever since she caught sight of the blood.

Tana hovered at the foot of the bed, looking ready to intervene if necessary. But Blair murmured to her quietly, and tried to lead her out of the room.

"We'll be in the cafeteria," Tana called over her shoulder, her expression still wary. "I can be right back here in less than two minutes if you need anything."

Sable nodded through her tears, then closed her eyes to cry quietly against Roman. He rubbed her back as she melted into his warmth.

After a minute, he spoke, voice rumbling in his chest beneath her ear. "Are you in pain?"

Her heart hurt so much that it took a moment for her to process how the rest of her body felt. "Not right now. I woke up with cramping, but that's…" The reality of the loss struck her like a blow. "The pain is gone now."

"What did the doctor say?" Roman tipped her chin up to look in her eyes.

He looked stressed. Harried. But the tender concern she saw in his gaze was so compassionate and kind that she had to remind herself it wasn't for her so much as their baby.

"He called in a specialist. I'm waiting for an OB now." She swiped her wrist under her eyes and tried to straighten when she saw that she'd left a wet spot on his blue dress shirt. "Sorry to cry all over you."

He shook his head, as if to dismiss her apology. He smoothed his thumb along her temple, wiping away more tear tracks. "I'm the one who's sorry. I'm so damned sorry you're bearing this, Sable. The pain. The fear. I hate thinking about you waking up alone and hurting. I can't imagine how scared you were."

His regrets were so focused on her that she met his dark gaze again, trying to gauge what he was thinking.

"I know you love this baby as much as I do—" she began. But she couldn't finish.

"And I still do." He wrapped her in his arms and squeezed her, the scent and feel of him reminding her of all the times she'd been close to him. The times that had made her fall in love with him. He pressed a kiss into her hair. "But there's no reason to think you've already miscarried, is there? There's still a chance they'll say the baby is fine."

A fresh wave of sadness made her pull away, the hygienic pillowcase behind her back crinkling as she moved. "I don't think you should get your hopes up—"

"This isn't about my hopes, Sable." He gripped her shoulders, steadying her as if he could impress the words on her. "I just want you to be healthy and well. I know how much the last miscarriage devastated you, and I'd do anything to ensure you never feel that kind of hurt again."

The sentiment behind the heartfelt words was reflected in his eyes. Or was that wishful thinking on her part, born out of a need to be loved by him?

While she wondered about it, a loudspeaker nearby crackled to life with a code message, the speaker's voice urgent. Outside the ER room, she could hear a rush of footsteps as medical professionals scrambled to answer the summons. After a moment, she recalled Roman's words.

Along with her sense that he might have cared more for her than she'd realized.

"But you really wanted this baby," she reminded him, unwilling to get tangled up in her love for Roman. He'd already made it clear he wouldn't return her feelings. "I know your hopes were high, too. I could see it in your eyes both times I had the ultrasounds."

"Being a father was a gift I didn't think I'd ever

have." He reached behind her to adjust the pillows before coaxing her to lie back against the raised bed. Then he smoothed her hair from her face, his dark gaze roaming over her features. "You stirred that hope in me, Sable. Not just because you're pregnant. You made me feel deeply again. Being with you made me long for a life I thought I'd turned my back on forever."

Her heart skipped a beat, the tempo feeling as off-kilter as she did. "But at the park yesterday, when we talked about the future—"

"I'm so ashamed of myself for not recognizing that I loved you before now, Sable, but I—"

"What?" Her question was barely a breath of sound, but he must have heard it because he squeezed her hands in his.

And repeated the words she feared she'd dreamed.

"I love you, Sable. I didn't allow myself to acknowledge it because I told myself that I was dead inside after Annette died." The bleak sorrow she remembered from the day at the Cloisters was there in his eyes again, but it was tempered with a different look now. Regret. "I'm so sorry I refused to see what was right in front of my eyes all along. But after I went home yesterday "

The door to the exam room burst open, and in the next instant, a tall Latina woman in a lab coat was striding straight to the bed. "Ms. Cordero, I'm

Dr. Incarnacion." Behind the doctor, a nurse rolled in a cart with a small machine. "I read your doctor's notes from your ultrasound earlier today, and based on the baby's activity at that time, I hope you're just experiencing some first trimester cervical bleeding. I brought the fetal Doppler with me so we can listen to the baby's heartbeat to learn more."

The woman's calm demeanor steadied her, even though she could see the nurse was working quickly to set up the Doppler machine. Vaguely, she heard Roman introduce himself while the doctor dragged a stool to the foot of the bed to perform her own exam.

Sable's thoughts were still half on her interrupted conversation with Roman. He'd said he loved her. The certainty in his voice still hummed inside her, a resonant echo that gave her new courage for facing whatever came next, even though she didn't fully understand what had changed his mind.

Hearing he loved her—knowing she hadn't given her heart unwisely—healed something inside her. Helped her let go of the past that had weighed on her shoulders for too long.

The need to take comfort from that love made her thread her fingers through his while they waited for the doctor's prognosis.

"Are you okay?" Roman shifted so he faced her fully, his dark eyes filled with concern that she now understood wasn't just about their baby after all.

And for a moment, she thought that maybe she could be okay. Even if she wasn't able to carry this tiny life to full term, the caring etched in the lines around Roman's eyes told her that she wouldn't be alone in the aftermath. He wouldn't leave her if she didn't have this baby.

Because this man's love was deep and true, and he didn't give it lightly.

Before she could answer him, however, the Doppler machine broadcast the sound of a strong, rapid heartbeat. With the volume cranked up high, that steady and insistent pulsing filled the whole room.

Filled all the spaces of her heart that weren't already taken up by Roman.

Relief flooded Roman.

Not just because he already loved the child Sable carried. But because he'd been scared out of his mind over what the loss of another baby would do to the woman who meant more to him than anything.

The joy he saw in her hazel eyes now was the most beautiful thing he'd ever seen, making him all the more committed to moving heaven and earth to keep that expression there as often as it was in his power to do so. And, far from feeling disloyal to his dead wife, he breathed in a deep certainty that he was—at long last—at peace with her loss. Annette would have wanted him to be happy and live fully.

He'd always known that on a rational level. It had been his own need to prove his devotion to her that had kept him from admitting what he felt for Sable.

What he had now was every bit as deep and intense. Now that he'd embraced those feelings, he finally honored Annette's love of life better than he'd been able to over the last five unhappy years.

Still holding Sable's hands, Roman lifted each to his lips in turn, kissing the backs of them while the doctor assured them their baby was thriving and that the bleeding was likely from the internal exam performed earlier yesterday. Nevertheless, Roman quizzed the physician about signs to look for in the days ahead, even asking if he should purchase their own fetal heart monitor for at-home use if it could give Sable peace of mind.

"It's very rare that I recommend them for in-home use," the doctor explained while she washed and dried her hands at the sink off to one side of the exam room. "The risk of side effects is minuscule in the hands of a trained technician, but unless they're medically needed, I don't recommend my patients use them. You can certainly check with her physician, however."

Roman made a mental note to do just that. And to read as much as possible about keeping Sable safe.

For now, he just hoped he would have the chance to show her how much he loved her and wanted her in his life. Their conversation had been interrupted earlier, even if it was for the very best of news.

"Is it safe to take her home?" he asked while Sable texted the friends who'd brought her to the emergency room.

Friends he needed to thank profusely. Both for their fast thinking and their vigilance in watching over her.

"Yes. Just make sure she gets adequate rest." The woman turned to the laptop a nurse slid in front of her, and she began typing notes on the keyboard. "She should check in with her doctor tomorrow, and I'll send her records from this visit. But I would be surprised if they need to see her before the next regularly scheduled appointment. Your baby looks very healthy."

With that, the woman and the nurse departed, leaving Sable to dress.

And leaving Roman unsure how to proceed.

Should he let her leave with her friends and ask to see her once she was better rested? If he didn't think it might upset her, he would ask her to return home with him now where he could watch over her personally.

Damn, but he regretted not being able to finish their talk earlier. Would she even believe him now? Believe that he loved her for her own sake and not just as the carrier of his child? He ached at all the words still left unsaid. And he hated that it had taken him this long to realize how devastated he would be to lose this woman.

"Sable." The word was cracked and raw, just like his emotions.

She glanced up at him, pausing in the act of tugging a plastic bag of her belongings from a shelf near the hospital bed. Her expression fell as she saw his face, which no doubt reflected the fear taking hold of him.

But the door to the room flew open again, this time admitting her girlfriends—the tall, elegant blonde, and the petite dynamo with rainbow-colored hair who'd tried to keep him from entering the room when he first got there.

The women swooped in with arms outstretched, folding Sable into hugs between them with so much love that it made him remember how slow he'd been to offer his own.

With regret burning a hole in him, he backed up a step.

"Can I come by tomorrow? After you've had a chance to rest?" It hurt to walk away. But it was his fault that he'd thrown every barrier imaginable in the way of loving her.

"Of course." She nodded, and although she still smiled, she looked a little puzzled at his retreat.

Or was that sheer hopefulness on his part?

"Until tomorrow, then." He turned his attention to her friends. "Ladies, I can't thank you enough for taking care of her. Will you be okay getting her home? I can give you a ride—"

"We're fine," the dynamo assured him, pale gray eyes turning steely as she looked his way. "She's in the best possible hands."

The emphasis on *the best* let him know where he ranked in the woman's eyes.

But since dawn would be breaking any minute, he wasn't going to argue with her. Bottom line, Sable needed her sleep as per doctor's orders.

Still, he was surprised the rainbow-haired pixie followed him to the door to see him out of the room while Sable's other friend helped her into a pair of sweatpants.

"If you're not going to bring your A game to wooing Sable tomorrow, don't bother showing up at the brownstone," the friend warned him in a low voice as he stepped out into the corridor.

Roman's respect for her climbed another notch.

"I'll be there," he assured her. "I'm going to lay the whole world at her feet."

The woman's eyes took his measure for a long moment, her somber gray gaze unwavering, but in the end, she cracked a smile that transformed her whole face. "Good luck, then, Daddy-to-be. You've got your work cut out for you."

Thirteen

Feet propped on pillows, Sable reclined on a patio lounger in the garden behind the brownstone later that day when she heard a man's voice inside the house.

Roman?

Her hopes soared unchecked after his declaration of love at the hospital. And even though she wasn't entirely sure why he'd given her over to the care of her friends so readily after sharing that he loved her, she trusted him to know his own heart. She understood him well enough to know those words hadn't been said lightly.

She'd thought about him to the point of distraction ever since she'd awoken a little past noon, well rested and no longer bleeding. She'd phoned her doctor's office right after waking, but her OB hadn't deemed it necessary for her to come in, assuring her that she could continue with her normal activity.

After showering and checking in with her mother via text, Sable had come downstairs to be greeted by a flurry of admonishments from Blair and Tana, who'd insisted on serving her a late breakfast in the courtyard where they'd toted blankets and pillows to make her comfortable.

All in all, she'd been thoroughly spoiled. The only thing missing was Roman.

Until now.

He emerged from the house dressed in dark pants and loafers, the sleeves of his pale gray Henley shirt rolled up in a way that showed off his forearms. She hadn't seen him dressed casually very often and today he appeared…delectable. He was clean-shaven in a way that told her he'd showered recently; she'd noticed before how a shadow of scruff covered his jaw within hours of a shave. Thinking about it made her want to trail her lips over his cheek to test the smoothness for herself.

"You look beautiful," he told her in lieu of a greeting, the serious undertone of the words making her think he'd been perusing her as intently as she'd been checking him out.

The thought made her hopes—already fizzy and light—lift off even higher. Behind him, she noticed shadows move in the windows of the dining room on the garden level of the brownstone. She smiled to think that her friends were keeping tabs on her. No doubt they felt a little protective after the way she'd cried her eyes out the day before when she'd returned from the Central Park outing with Roman.

But things had shifted dramatically between them at the hospital. Over the late breakfast with her friends this morning, she'd told Tana and Blair about Roman's declaration of love. Blair had squealed with unchecked approval. Tana had told her that anyone could throw around words like "love," but only special people backed up the idea with actions.

If anything, the words only underscored for Sable that she'd already seen so many acts that spoke of love. Of Roman's need to care for her and provide for her, his insistence that she think about a future beyond motherhood to ensure her happiness.

"Thank you. I feel much better." She watched as Roman drew a second padded patio lounger closer over the gray-and-white striped outdoor rug and seated himself on the edge of the chair to face her. Now that he was closer, she noticed the shadows under his eyes. "You look tired. Did you have trouble sleeping?"

Birds chirped in the ornamental trees planted around the courtyard, the nearby buildings dulling the sounds of traffic from DeKalb Avenue along Fort Greene Park.

"I'm okay. Better now that I can see for myself you've recovered nicely since I saw you at the hospital." His expression was troubled. "I've spent all the time since then thinking about how to convince you—"

He broke off, shaking his head as if frustrated.

"What? How to convince me of what?" Alarmed that he seemed worried, she shifted on her bed of pillows so she could take his hand.

"I'm going about this all wrong." He stared down at the place where her fingers gripped his. He stroked his thumb over hers, capturing it beneath his. "I came here today with a car and driver waiting out front, thinking I'd give you a tour of all the best options for you to consider for a home." He huffed out a long breath.

"Really?" Curious, she wondered if he still wanted her input on a place for himself. She liked the idea of him having his own place in New York with room for their child.

And maybe, one day, room for her, too. Suddenly,

that was a very real possibility now that he had feelings for her.

"Yes. And we can still do that." He gave a clipped nod, but his gaze remained anxious. "But now that I see you, all I can think about is how to make you believe that I love you, Sable. Even if the worst had happened last night, I would still be right here today, asking you for another chance to prove how much you mean to me. For another chance to make you happy."

Her heart swelled. She sat up enough to cup his jaw with her free hand, testing the smoothness of his jaw with her fingers.

"You *are* making me happy, just by being here and caring about what I need." She felt his love and concern wrap around her as tangibly as a hug. Her whole marriage had never given her as much security as she felt just from Roman's one declaration of love. "And how could I doubt that you love me after you told me as much? I know too well you would have never said the words unless you meant them. Look how well you loved the last woman who held your heart."

His heavy shoulders relaxed a fraction, some of the concern in his eyes dissolving. He clasped a hand around hers where she cupped his face, and he turned his lips into her palm to kiss it.

Pleasure shivered over her skin. Joy shimmered in her soul.

"I didn't know if you would trust what I said when I was so adamant about keeping that torch for her." His voice was pitched low, the words rough-edged as if he hadn't ever planned to share them. "But she would have never wanted me to grieve that way. She spelled it out for me, actually, before she went into surgery that last time. She wanted me to promise I'd find happiness no matter what happened. But I was so adamant about ignoring what she said, so certain she'd come through."

Needing to offer him comfort, Sable slid from her lounger to climb into his lap. "It must have been so painful for you."

Strong arms held her tighter. "I thought I was being strong for her by discounting what she said. It turned out, she was the strong one. I just wasn't ready to hear what she said until yesterday. I came home from the park, and the memories of what she said—of everything that was important to her—just came flooding over me and I knew how deeply I'd messed up with you. I felt like she was right there telling me not to be an idiot. To go get you and our child and live our dreams."

Sable kissed his cheek. His lips. She shed a few happy tears in between kisses, unspeakably grateful to have his loyal, passionate heart to call her own.

"You have me, Roman," she promised, pausing the trail of kisses long enough to meet his dark eyes. "You have my body, and my heart, and all my love. You've had them ever since you undressed me that night in the studio, even though I kept trying to tell myself it was just physical." A smile curved her mouth, the happiness inside her bubbling over. "My heart knew better the whole time."

"After how stubborn and blind I've been, I'm not sure I deserve you." Frowning, he traced the fullness of her lower lip with his thumb. "I resigned my position as head of the equity firm, by the way. So on top of being stubborn and blind, I'm most likely disinherited. But I wanted to show Marcel my love and support in no uncertain terms. You were right about that."

"Good for you." A different kind of pleasure filled her. "Does that mean you want to relocate to New York full-time?" It hadn't occurred to her until now that he had worked hard to help other people—guiding the business end of Marcel's company, taking the reins for his grandfather and caring for his wife when her health failed. But who worked to bring comfort and ease to Roman's life?

She could do that for him. She welcomed the chance to be there for him the way he wanted to be there for her. A partnership. Something she'd never had before.

Something that was now possible because of this amazing man who'd taken her life by storm.

"I'm keeping a toehold in Los Angeles for when you're ready to move your celebrity stylist business to the West Coast." Leaning back in the lounger with her still in his lap, he shifted position so they reclined together, her leg straddling his in a way that stirred a new heat. "Besides, I might have clients who'll want to come with me if I decide to do any private investing. For the next year, though, I'm going to put all my focus on helping Marcel launch a storefront. I found out this morning our bid was accepted on a property on Broome Street."

"Get out!" Excitement stirred at the thought of a flagship store happening so quickly for Zayn Designs. She levered herself up on her elbow, propping herself on his broad chest. "Can we see it?"

"I do have that car waiting to take you house hunting," he reminded her. His hand resting on her waist ventured lower, curling around her hip. Squeezing her curves. "There's a brownstone near Prospect Park that just came on the market if you want to stay in Brooklyn, for that matter."

Wow. He really meant what he said. He'd been planning.

The idea of being close to her friends tempted her, but the warmth of his palm refocused her attention on the proximity of his hard body. She arched her back in a way that lifted her breasts closer to his mouth while pressing the juncture of her legs against his thigh.

"How long will your driver wait?" she inquired, her fingers tracing his collarbone just inside the lightweight cotton of his shirt.

Roman's eyes flamed. He gripped her more securely in a way that caused her to rub against him. "Long enough for you to give me a tour of your bedroom."

An empty ache inside her made her wriggle impatiently. "You read my mind. I've been wanting to show it to you."

"And what do you know, I've been dying to make you feel good."

Sable kissed him, long and deep, tongues tangling until they were both breathless. She tried to pull away enough to stand up, but he tugged her off her feet and carried her through the garden toward the back door.

"We're going to make *each other* feel good," she clarified when she recovered the power to speak.

"And then, we're going to make each other happy for a long, long time to come." He stared down at her with dark eyes full of promise, a future written there that made her a little giddy and a whole lot satisfied.

She didn't bother trying to reply, though. Wind-

ing her arms around his neck, she lost herself in the
kiss and the certainty they were going to make all
their dreams come true.

Epilogue

Ten months later

Tucking his four-month-old daughter into the crook of one arm, Roman pushed open the double doors to Zayn Designs with the other, eager to deliver his sweetly fretful little charge to her mama.

Not that he minded settling Leyla down when she fussed. He took it as a personal endorsement of his parenting skills that he could distract his baby girl even better than the nanny, who would arrive at the new store within the hour to take Leyla home.

"You're here!" Sable's happy voice greeted him

even before he saw her in the small crowd of after-party guests Marcel had invited for the grand opening.

Dressed in a silk slip dress that hugged her newly voluptuous curves, she waved Roman over to a corner near a freestanding bar, where she was flanked by Marcel and Cybil Deschamps.

After eight months of construction and two more months of interior design, Zayn Designs had opened for business today. And while Sable had long ago completed her internship for the company, Marcel had recently enticed her back part-time as an assistant to the creative director. The opportunity had come just in time for New York Fashion Week in February, when Leyla was two months old.

By now, Leyla was used to her mother's schedule, and Roman didn't mind ferrying his daughter around when she needed to be breastfed. Having the chance to sit with the two people he loved most in the world was the best part of his day.

"Hello, beautiful girl." He greeted his wife with a kiss before saying hello to Marcel and Cybil. "How's it going?"

Cybil, decked out in the Zayn Designs brand to support the store, wrapped an arm around Sable's shoulders. "Sable is making waves with her social media photos from the grand opening. She already got Zayn some celebrity endorsements and reposts."

As Sable lifted Leyla from his arms, the baby seemed to remember she was famished and let out a wail. Murmuring her excuses, Sable started for the back room. Roman began to follow her when his brother fell into step beside him.

"It's pretty convenient how you can make her cry on cue to get your wife alone," Marcel observed before clamping a hand on Roman's arm and bringing him to a halt in a quiet corner of the store. "We got calls from around the globe today, Roman. Orders from London, Paris and Milan. A few from Singapore and Dubai. One of the Dubai customers asked if she could invest in a storefront over there to facilitate our getting into the market."

Marcel's excitement was palpable as he stood there surrounded by the results of his hard work. A champagne bottle popped behind the bar as the caterers passed drinks to the guests hand-selected for the after-party. The lighting highlighted the clothes like fine art against the walls, which were also covered with paintings that Marcel had personally chosen. Everything about the restrained elegance of the space reflected his brother's keen eye and good taste, and it did Roman's heart proud to see Marcel's efforts rewarded and embraced.

"Wow. That's incredible." Impressed, Roman clapped him on the shoulder. "Congratulations, Marcel. You deserve every accolade that's coming your way, and more. You've done great work here."

"Me?" Marcel shook his head, dark hair falling in one eye. "*We* did great work. The Zayn brothers. With the help of one very talented newcomer to the clan."

Roman grinned at the way he included Sable in the family. Roman had convinced her to marry him in a courthouse ceremony last fall before Leyla was born, but they had plans to exchange vows on the beach in Malibu over the summer in a ceremony with their closest friends and family. Sable had been to the Malibu house with him twice. She'd fallen in love with the ocean views and looked forward to spending more time there soon.

"I don't know about Dubai, but I'll look into it. Next up is Los Angeles, then Miami." He had a solid business plan in place, but if sales were as strong as Marcel hinted, maybe they'd accelerate the timeline. Capitalize on the momentum.

He hadn't gone back to Zayn Equity, even when his grandfather had suggested a family meeting to iron out their differences. Roman had recognized that he enjoyed working with his brother far more, and he appreciated the additional time it allowed him to spend with his wife and daughter.

Ever since he'd promised his love to Sable, he'd

been on a mission to enjoy life and the good things that came his way. And life was very, very good.

"Of course." Marcel nodded, content to give Roman free rein to handle the business the same way Roman gave his brother control of the creative end. "I hope you know Sable can head home whenever she wants. The party won't run late. I'm just glad to have seen you both tonight to celebrate the success."

"The nanny will be here shortly to take Leyla home," Roman assured him, his gaze darting to the door to the back room where Sable was feeding the baby. "Sable and I both want to stay a while to celebrate the first of many new milestones."

"Good." Marcel lifted a champagne glass in a silent toast. "Find me before you leave so we can have a real drink."

Agreeing to that plan, Roman opened the door to the small employee break room at the back of the shop. He didn't see Sable, but heard her call from down the hall.

"Roman? I'm back here."

Following the sound of her voice, he reached the storage area where Marcel had left a new sofa that hadn't worked in the store's interior design. Surrounded by rolling racks of clothes, Sable was tucked into a corner of the white leather, a layette blanket covering half her dress. She'd tugged off a strap to free one breast, and cradled their baby close.

"I'm so glad you brought her." Sable smiled up at him, maternal contentment glowing in her lovely face. "My breasts were killing me."

"They're killing me, too," he assured her, taking the seat beside her so he could wrap his arm around her as securely as she held their little girl. "You're more gorgeous every day."

"Mmm." She tipped her head against his chest, nuzzling into him. "So are you. Seeing you carry my baby around is the sexiest thing ever."

"One of many reasons I like being a dad." He pressed a kiss into the top of her hair. "I see that hungry gleam in your eye whenever I show off my parenting prowess."

He cupped her elbow just beneath the spot where Leyla's head rested. Already the little girl's eyes were closing, her rosebud lips loosening from Sable's nipple.

"This day has been so perfect," she said on a soft sigh, trailing her fingers over Leyla's cheek. "The store is a success. My baby is happy and healthy. I'm wildly in love. And soon I'll get to go home with you and show you how much."

Roman shifted her in his arms just enough so that he could look down into her hazel eyes. She was his temptress. His lover. His wife. He'd never imagined his life could be this full, his heart this complete.

"If it's even half how much I love you, I'm the luckiest man alive."

* * * * *

If you loved
Sable and Roman,
don't miss Blair's story,
Ways to Tempt the Boss,
by USA TODAY *bestselling author*
Joanne Rock.
Available September 2021
from Harlequin Desire.

WE HOPE YOU ENJOYED
THIS BOOK FROM

DESIRE

Luxury, scandal, desire—welcome to
the lives of the American elite.

Be transported to the worlds of oil barons, family dynasties, moguls and celebrities. Get ready for juicy plot twists, delicious sensuality and intriguing scandal.

6 NEW BOOKS AVAILABLE EVERY MONTH!

#2815 TRAPPED WITH THE TEXAN
Texas Cattleman's Club: Heir Apparent • by Joanne Rock
To start her own horse rescue, Valencia Donovan needs the help of wealthy rancher Lorenzo Cortez-Williams. It's all business between them despite how handsome he is. But when they're forced to take shelter together during a tornado, there's no escaping the heat between them...

#2816 GOOD TWIN GONE COUNTRY
Dynasties: Beaumont Bay • by Jessica Lemmon
Straitlaced Hallie Banks is nothing like her superstar twin sister, Hannah. But she wants to break out of her shell. Country bad boy Gavin Sutherland is the one who can teach her how. But will one hot night turn into more than fun and games?

#2817 HOMECOMING HEARTBREAKER
Moonlight Ridge • by Joss Wood
Mack Holloway hasn't been home in years. Now he's back at his family's luxury resort to help out—and face the woman he left behind. Molly Haskell hasn't forgiven him, but they'll soon discover the line between hate and passion is very thin...

#2818 WHO'S THE BOSS NOW?
Titans of Tech • by Susannah Erwin
When tech tycoon Evan Fletcher finds Marguerite Delacroix breaking into his newly purchased winery, he doesn't turn her in—he offers her a job. As hard as they try to keep things professional, their chemistry is undeniable...until secrets about the winery change everything!

#2819 ONE MORE SECOND CHANCE
Blackwells of New York • by Nicki Night
A tropical destination wedding finds exes Carter Blackwell and maid of honor Phoenix Jones paired during the festivities. The charged tension between them soon turns romantic, but will the problems of their past get in the way of a second chance at forever?

#2820 PROMISES FROM A PLAYBOY
Switched! • by Andrea Laurence
After a plane crash on a secluded island leaves Finn Steele with amnesia, local resident Willow Bates gives him shelter. Sparks fly as they're secluded together, but will their connection be enough to weather the revelations of his wealthy playboy past?

HDCNM0721

"Listen." Carter broke the silence when they reached her door. "I didn't mean to upset you."

Phoenix cut him off. "Don't worry about it."

"I thought the timing was right. We were getting along and…"

"It's evident you still have an issue with timing," Phoenix snapped.

Her comment stung. Carter took a deep breath and exhaled slowly. He tried not to lose his patience with her.

"I'm sorry. I shouldn't have said that." Phoenix carefully stepped over the threshold and turned back toward Carter.

"I'm sorry, too. Hopefully we can move on. It was nice being friendly. Maybe one day we could go back to that."

Phoenix looked away. When she looked back at Carter, there was something unreadable in her eyes. Had she been more affected by his news than he realized? Their eyes locked. Carter felt himself moving closer to her.

"We just need to get through the wedding tomorrow and the next few days, and we can go back to living our normal lives.

You won't have to see me and I won't have to see you."

Phoenix's words struck something in him. He didn't like the idea of never seeing her again. The past few days had awakened something in him. Even the tense moments reminded him of what he once loved about her. He remembered his own words… *The way I love you.*

Carter kept his eyes on hers. She held his gaze. Old feelings returned, stirring his emotions. Perhaps those feelings had never left and remained dormant in his soul. His heart quickened. Desire flooded him and he wondered what Phoenix would do if he kissed her. She still hadn't looked away. Was she waiting for him to leave? Did she want to kiss him as much as he wanted to kiss her? Maybe she was having some of the same wild thoughts. Maybe old feelings were coming to the surface for her, too.

Carter stepped closer to Phoenix. She didn't move. Carter noticed the rise and fall of her chest become more intense. He stepped closer. She stayed put. He watched her throat shift as she swallowed. He smelled the sweet scent of perfume. He wondered if he could taste the salt on her skin.

Carter wasn't sure if it was love, but he felt something. It was more than lust. He missed Phoenix. The thought of her absence burned in him. In this moment he realized every woman since her had been an attempted replacement. That's why none of those relationships worked. But Phoenix would never have him. Would she?

Don't miss what happens next in…
One More Second Chance *by Nicki Night.*

*Available August 2021 wherever
Harlequin Desire books and ebooks are sold.*

Harlequin.com

*Can wallflower Iris Daniels heal the heart of
Gold Valley's most damaged cowboy?*

Read on for a sneak peek at
The Heartbreaker of Echo Pass,
the brand-new Western romance by New York Times
bestselling author Maisey Yates!

Iris Daniels wondered if there was a particular art to
changing your life. If so, then she wanted to find it. If so,
she needed to. Because she'd about had enough of her
quiet baking-and-knitting existence.

Not that she'd had enough of baking and knitting. She
loved both things.

Like she loved her family.

But over the last couple of months, she had been turning
over a plan to reorder her life.

It had all started when her younger sister, Rose, had tried
to set her up with a man who was the human equivalent of
a bowl of oatmeal.

Iris didn't like to be mean, but it was the truth.

Iris, who had never gone on a date in her life, had been
swept along in her younger sister's matchmaking scheme.
The only problem? Elliott hadn't liked her at all.

Elliott had liked Rose.

And Iris didn't know what bothered her more. That her
sister had only been able to imagine her with a man when
he was so singularly beige, or that Iris had allowed herself
to get swept along with it in the first place.

Not only get swept along with it, but get to the point where she had convinced herself that it was a good thing. That she should perhaps make a real effort to get this guy to like her because no one else ever had.

That maybe Elliott, who liked to talk about water filtration like some people talked about sports, their children or once-in-a-lifetime vacations, was the grandest adventure she would ever go on.

That she had somehow imagined that for her, dating a man who didn't produce any sort of spark in her at all, simply because he was there, was adventure.

That she had been almost eager to take any attention she could, the idea of belonging to someone, feeling special, was so intoxicating she had ignored reality, ignored so many things, to try to spin a web of lies to make herself feel better.

That had been some kind of rock bottom. Truly terrifying.

It was one thing to let yourself get swept away in a tide of years that passed without you noticing, as things around you changed and you were there, inevitably the same.

It was quite another to be complicit in your own underwhelming life. To have willingly decided to be grateful for something she hadn't even wanted.

Don't miss
The Heartbreaker of Echo Pass
by New York Times *bestselling author Maisey Yates,
available July 2021 wherever Harlequin books and
ebooks are sold.*

HQNBooks.com